LOVE LI

(THE ROMANCE CHRONICLES—BOOK 1)

SOPHIE LOVE

CHAPTER ONE

Keira Swanson pushed open the glass doors of *Viatorum* magazine and walked purposefully inside. It was Labor Day, but she, along with the rest of the writing staff, had been summoned to work at short notice.

Keira knew full well there was no real emergency, nothing big enough to trigger a summoning on a public holiday. But the travel magazine was a hugely competitive environment and her boss, Joshua, liked to "create opportunities to weed out the weak." Anyone who kicked up too much of a fuss about working on a holiday or looked too miserable during their meetings would find themselves swiftly unemployed. Keira had fought so hard for a writing job, she wasn't about to fail at this hurdle, even if it did mean leaving her boyfriend, Zachary, at home to host a family brunch without her.

Her black stilettos click-clacked across the pristine, white tiles as she hurried to her desk. The *Viatorum* HQ was located in the hippest part of New York City, in a huge, old warehouse that had been stylishly repurposed for office use. The windows were enormous, stretching all the way from the floor to the steepled ceiling, where steel beams with large bolts were still in place from the days when it had been used as a warehouse. The open-plan environment meant that every conversation was heard. Even whispers echoed. It also meant that no one dared bring in anything too pungent for lunch. Keira could still recall the moment a new writer, a ditzy young woman named Abby, had brought in a tuna salad on her first day. The second Joshua had caught a whiff of it he'd quickly ensured it was Abby's first, last, and only day at *Viatorum.*

Peering across the vast room, Keira noticed that she wasn't the first to arrive. Nina, her friend and one of the assistant editors at *Viatorum,* was already hunched over her desk, tapping away at her keyboard. She flashed Keira a quick grin before reimmersing herself in her work.

Keira slung her purse down on her desk and slumped into her chair, careful to make her sigh inaudible. She hadn't realized working at the prestigious *Viatorum* magazine would involve so much acting, so much faking interest in conversation, so much pretending to be oh-so-accomplished.

1

Through the glass partition that separated Joshua from his employees, Keira realized that he was watching her. She wondered what he was thinking, whether he was surprised to see that she was the second person who had responded to his urgent summoning, or whether he was on the hunt to fire someone and she'd just become the prey that had wandered into his territory.

Joshua emerged around the glass partition. He was wearing an electric blue suit and his hair was styled into a quiff. He stalked up to Keira's desk.

"Have you finished the Ireland research yet?" he asked, not even bothering to say hello.

Ah yes, the Festival of Love article that Joshua had been assigned to write by Elliot, the CEO of *Viatorum*. It was supposed to be a huge, important project—at least that's what Joshua had insinuated—though Keira herself couldn't fathom how a silly fluff piece on matchmaking during an outdated ceremony in a quaint Irish village could be construed as important. Even so, Joshua had been in an even fouler mood than usual and, as his most junior writer, Keira had been tasked with doing all the research he was "far too busy" to do himself.

More like far too self-important, Keira thought silently to herself, as she looked up and smiled. "I emailed it to you before I left on Friday."

"Email it to me again," Joshua demanded without missing a beat. "I don't have time to trawl through my inbox looking for it."

"No problem," Keira said, remaining as cordial as ever.

Joshua stormed back to his office and Keira pinged the email containing the vast amount of information she'd gathered on the Irish Festival of Love over to him, smirking to herself as she recalled how silly it all was, how sickeningly *romantic.*

No sooner had the email left her inbox than the doors swung open and a handful of *Viatorum*'s writing staff bustled in, each pretending they weren't peeved to be in the office on what was supposed to be a national vacation. Keira could hear their chatter as they tried to outdo one another with their sacrifices.

"My niece was competing in a baseball tournament," Lisa said. "But this is much more important. She cried her eyes out when I said I was leaving but I know she'll understand when she's old enough and has her own career."

Duncan was not to be outdone. "I had to leave Stacy at the airport. I mean, we can visit Madrid another time, it's not like it's going anywhere."

"I just left my mother's hospital bed," Victoria added. "It's not like she's critical or anything. She understands my career comes first."

Keira kept her smirk to herself. The corporate environment at *Viatorum* seemed completely unnecessary to her. She wished her career could develop through dedication, skill, and hard work, rather than through her adeptness at schmoozing by the water cooler. That wasn't to say Keira wasn't focused on her career—it was the most important thing to her in her life at the moment, though she wouldn't admit that to Zachary—she just didn't want to change herself to fit into the culture at the magazine. She often felt like she was biding her time, waiting for her moment to shine.

A second later Keira's phone buzzed. Nina had sent her one of her covert messages.

I'm guessing Joshua hasn't prepared you for the fact that Elliot's coming in for this meeting.

Keira held in her gasp of surprise. Though the CEO at *Viatorum* was a million times more pleasant than Joshua, she felt more anxious when in his presence. He held the key to the future of her career. He was the one with the power to hire and fire on the spot, the one whose opinion really mattered. Joshua would never tell Keira if she'd done good work, or that her writing had improved, no matter how hard she'd worked. Elliot, on the other hand, gave compliments when they were deserved, which was rarely, but that made it even better to get one.

Keira was about to text Nina back when she heard the sound of Joshua's fast footsteps approaching.

"What the hell is this crap, Keira?" he shouted before he'd even reached her desk.

His words echoed around the office. All heads turned to watch the most recent verbal bashing, simultaneously glad they weren't on the receiving end of it and excited by the prospect that some other sacrificial lamb would satisfy Joshua's urge to fire.

"I'm sorry?" Keira asked pleasantly, although her heart was racing.

"That crap about Ireland! All of it's useless!"

Keira wasn't sure how to respond. She knew she'd done good research; she'd kept to specification, she'd presented her findings in a user-friendly document, she'd gone above and beyond. Joshua was just in a foul mood and taking it out on her. If anything, this was a test to see how she would respond to a public verbal bashing.

"I can do some further research if you'd like," Keira said.

"There's not enough time!" Joshua yelled. "Elliot will be here in fifteen minutes!"

"Actually," Nina interrupted, "his car just pulled up." She leaned over in her office chair, taking in the sight from the large window.

Joshua turned bright red. "I'm not taking the rap for this, Swanson," he said, pointing at Keira. "If Elliot's disappointed I'll let him know where the blame lies."

He went to stomp back to his partitioned desk. But as he went, one of his patent-leather brogues landed right on top of a puddle of coffee one of his harried, rushed writers had spilled on the tiled floors in their haste to get to work.

There was a moment of suspended animation, where Keira could sense that a terrible event was about to unfold. Then it started, Joshua's cartoon-like sliding and stumbling motions. He twisted his torso as though in a strange dance as he tried to keep his balance. But the combination of granite tiles and macchiato was too great to overcome.

Joshua lost his footing completely, one leg shooting forward while the other twisted oddly beneath him. Everyone gasped as he landed heavily and loudly on the hard floor. A crunch noise rang out through the huge office, echoing sickeningly.

"My leg!" Joshua screamed, clutching his shin through his electric blue pants. "I've broken my leg!"

Everyone seemed stunned into paralysis. Keira ran up to him, not sure what to do to help, but certain that breaking one's leg in such a manner had to be impossible.

"It won't be broken," she stammered, trying to be reassuring. But that was before her gaze fell to the awkward angle of Joshua's leg, to the tear in his pants through which she saw protruding bone. Nausea gripped her. "Actually…"

"Don't just stand there!" Joshua screamed at her, rolling around in agony. Through a squinting eye he stole a glance at his injury. "Oh God!" he screamed. "I've ripped my pants! These cost me more than you earn in a month!"

Just then, the main glass doors swung open and in strode Elliot.

Even if Elliot hadn't been six foot three he'd have been imposing. There was something about him, about the way he held himself. He could strike terror and obedience into people with just one glance.

Like deer caught in headlights, everyone stopped what they were doing and stared at him in fear. Even Joshua was scared into silence.

Elliot took in the sight before him; of Joshua lying on the ground, clutching his leg, screaming in pain; of Keira standing helplessly over him; of the crowd of writers standing at their desks with horrified expressions on their faces.

But Elliot's expression didn't change at all. "Has someone called an ambulance for Joshua?" was all he said.

There was a sudden flurry of movement.

"I'll do it!" everyone began saying over the top of one another as they clambered for their desk phones, desperate to be seen as the savior in front of Elliot.

A sheen of cold sweat glistened on Joshua's forehead. He looked up at Elliot.

"I'll be fine," he said through his clenched teeth, trying to sound nonchalant but failing miserably. "It's just a broken bone. Good thing it's my leg and not my arm. I don't need my leg to write the Ireland piece." He sounded somewhat delirious.

"But you do need it to get on a plane and trek around the hillsides," Elliot said calmly.

"Crutches," Joshua said, grimacing. "Wheelchair. We'll just need to adapt a bit."

"Joshua," Elliot replied, sternly, "the only place I'm sending you is the hospital."

"No!" Joshua cried, trying to sit up. "I can do the assignment! I just need a cast and then I'll be good as new!"

With no emotion at all, Elliot ignored Joshua's pleas and glanced at his watch. "I'm beginning the meeting at eleven sharp," he announced to the writing staff. Then he waltzed off to the conference room without so much as looking back.

Everyone stood there, silent, shocked, unsure what to do. Then Joshua's screaming snapped them back to attention.

"Let me get you some water," Lisa said.

"I don't want frickin' water!" Joshua yelled.

"Here," Duncan said, rushing forward. "You need to elevate the wound."

He reached for Joshua's damaged leg but Joshua smacked his arms away. "Don't touch me! I swear to God if you touch me I will fire you!"

Duncan drew back, hands in truce position.

"The ambulance is here," Nina called from the window, blue lights flashing from the other side.

Thank God, Keira thought. She'd had about as much of Joshua as she could stand for one day. For a lifetime, if she was being honest with herself.

Just then, she looked up and realized Elliot was standing in the doorway of the conference room, watching them all bustle around Joshua, acting like headless chickens. He looked less than impressed. Keira noticed the clock. The meeting was starting in less than one minute.

Keira realized there was an opportunity here. There was no way Joshua would be completing the Ireland assignment, Elliot had made that quite clear. Which meant everyone else would fight for it in order to get noticed. It wasn't the most glamorous of jobs but it was more than Keira had ever had. She needed to prove herself to Elliot. She needed that assignment.

Leaving her colleagues behind her, Keira strode toward the conference room. She passed Elliot in the doorway and took a seat next to the one she knew Elliot would soon be occupying.

Duncan noticed her first. Seeing her sitting in the empty conference room seemed to make it dawn on him suddenly what Keira herself had realized, that the Ireland assignment was vacant and one of them was needed to fill it. He rushed (while trying to hide the fact he was rushing) to be the next one inside. The others noticed, and there was a sudden scramble for the conference room, each colleague politely apologizing for "accidentally" shoving into the other in their haste to get inside, to impress Elliot, and to win the coveted assignment.

Which left Joshua completely alone in the middle of the open-plan office, paramedics hoisting him onto a gurney and stretchering him away, while a conference room full of his staff prepared themselves to battle it out for his assignment.

*

"I'm sure you've noticed by now," Elliot said, "that Joshua's unfortunate accident has left me in a bit of a predicament."

He folded his large hands on top of the conference table and glanced at all of the writers sitting in front of him.

Keira stayed quiet, biding her time. She had a strategy: let the others wear themselves out asking to be given the assignment and then swoop in at the last minute.

"The Ireland piece," Elliot continued, "was going to be our cover story. *Viatorum* is going in a new direction. Personal pieces, first-person accounts. The writer drives the narrative, creates a story, in which the location is a key character. I'd briefed Joshua on this. I don't know if any of you guys have the talent to do this, to understand my vision." He looked down at the tabletop, frowning so hard a vein bulged in his forehead. "The plane leaves tomorrow," he lamented, as though he didn't have an audience.

"If I may," Lisa said. "My Florida piece is almost done. I can finish it up on the plane."

"Absolutely not," Elliot replied. "No one can be on two assignments at once. Who's free?"

There was a collective deflating as several of the writers around the table realized that they were already out of the running.

"I'm free," Duncan said. "I was supposed to be flying to Madrid today but work comes first. Stacy won't mind if I defer the holiday."

Keira only just managed to stop herself from rolling her eyes on hearing Duncan's rehearsed line. She wondered how chill Stacy really was about her holiday being cancelled.

Elliot scrutinized Duncan across the table. "You're that Buxton guy, aren't you? The one who wrote the Frankfurt piece?"

"Yes," Duncan replied, grinning proudly.

"I hated that piece," Elliot said.

Keira could feel it bubbling up in her, the excitement. This was her moment. Her time to shine.

Ignoring the nerves she felt, she raised her hand with forced confidence. "I'm available for the piece."

Everyone's heads turned to look at her. She fought the urge to hunker down in her seat.

"Who are you?" Elliot asked.

Keira gulped. "Keira Swanson. I'm Joshua's junior writer. He tasked me to do some preliminary research for this piece."

"He did, did he?" Elliot asked, sounding unimpressed to learn that Joshua was dishing his duties out to his junior staff. He stroked his chin in contemplation. "You've not been abroad on an assignment before?"

Keira shook her head. "Not yet," she replied. "But I'm excited to." She hoped the warble in her voice couldn't be heard.

She could feel her colleagues around her bristling with irritation. They probably thought this was all very unfair, that Keira didn't deserve this assignment. They were probably kicking themselves for volunteering for less glamorous pieces in the weeks prior because now they were stuck with them. The only person showing any hint of support was Nina, who smiled in her knowing way. Internally, Keira felt herself smile as well. This was her moment. She'd been biding her time at *Viatorum*, mopping up after Joshua, rewriting his pieces on his behalf, working all hours with little reward. Now it was her turn in the spotlight.

Elliot drummed his fingers on the tabletop. "I'm not sure," he said. "You haven't proven yourself yet. And this is a big task."

Nina boldly piped up from the other end of the room. She'd done her time, earned trust and respect. Years of editing at high-end magazines had hardened her. "I don't think you have any other options."

Elliot paused as though letting the words sink in. Then his frown began to relax and with a reluctant sort of acceptance he said, "Fine. Swanson, you have the piece. But only because we're desperate."

It wasn't the best way in the world to receive such good news, but Keira didn't care. She'd gotten the piece. That was all that mattered. She had to fight the urge to punch the air.

"It's a four-week trip," Elliot explained. "To the Lisdoonvarna Festival, in Ireland."

Keira nodded; she already knew all of this. "The Festival of Love," she said wryly.

Elliot smirked. "So you're a cynic?"

Suddenly nervous, Keira worried whether she'd said the wrong thing, had let her disdain slip out by accident. But then she noticed Elliot's expression was actually one of approval.

"That's exactly the sort of angle I'm looking for," he said.

Everyone around the table looked like they'd sucked lemons. Lisa outright glared her jealousy at Keira.

"The truth," Elliot added, his eyes sparkling with sudden excitement. "I want you to debunk the silliness of the romance of Ireland. Debunk the myth that one can be matched with their life partner just through some sentimental festival. I need you to be brave and show how it's all nonsense, how love doesn't work like that in the real world. I want it warts and all."

Keira nodded. She was a cynical New Yorker, and the angle of the assignment sat very well with her. She couldn't help but feel like the perfect opportunity had landed in her lap at the perfect time. This was her chance to shine, to show off her voice and talent, to prove she deserved her place at *Viatorum.*

"Meeting dismissed," Elliot said. As Keira stood, he added, "Not you, Miss Swanson. We need to go through the finer details with my assistant. Please, let's head to my office."

As the others filed out of the conference room, Nina caught Keira's eye and flashed her a thumbs-up. Then Keira walked across the length of the office, side by side with Elliot, her heels clacking and drawing jealous stares from everyone around her.

The second the door shut to Elliot's office, Keira knew the real work was about to begin. Elliot's assistant, Heather, was already seated. She frowned with confusion when she realized Keira had been picked for the assignment, but she didn't say anything.

You're just another person to prove wrong, Keira thought.

She took her seat and so did Elliot. Heather handed a binder to her.

"Your plane tickets," she explained. "And details of your accommodations."

"I hope you're an early riser because you'll be leaving first thing in the morning," Elliot added.

Keira smiled, though her mind reeled through all of the planned events she had in her calendar, all the things she would have to cancel and miss out on. A cold sweat descended over her as she realized that she'd be missing Zachary's sister Ruth's wedding, which was the very next day. He was going to be so pissed!

"That's no problem," she said, looking down at the tickets in her binder that were for a 6 a.m. flight. "No problem at all."

"We've booked you into a quaint little B and B in Lisdoonvarna," Elliot explained. "No frills. We want you to experience everything."

"Great," she replied.

"Don't screw this up, okay?" Elliot said. "I'm taking a huge risk on you. If you mess this assignment up your days here are over. Got it? There's a hundred other writers waiting for your spot."

Keira nodded, trying not to show the anxiety on her face, trying to make herself look bold and confident and totally together, while inside, she felt as if a thousand butterflies had taken flight.

CHAPTER TWO

Later that evening, when Keira arrived back home to the apartment she shared with her boyfriend, she found herself still shaking with excitement and disbelief. Her hand trembled as she tried to get her key in the lock of their apartment door.

Finally, she opened the door and walked inside. The smell of cooked food lingered in the air, mixed with the smell of cleaning fluids. Zachary had been cleaning. That meant he was angry.

"I know, I know, I know," she began before he'd even come into her eye shot. "You're mad. And I'm sorry." She chucked her keys into the pot by the door and slammed the door shut. "But, babe, I have great news!" She slipped her heels off and rubbed her aching feet.

Zachary appeared in the doorway of the living room, his arms folded. His dark hair mirrored his dark expression.

"You missed brunch," he said. "The whole thing."

"I'm sorry!" Keira implored. She threw her arms around his neck but found he was resistant, so decided to change tack. She put on her sultry voice. "How about we argue about it and then I make it up to you?"

Zachary shoved her arms off of him and stomped into the living room, where he slumped onto the couch. The room was immaculately clean. Even his PlayStation had been dusted. He was more pissed off this time than ever, Keira realized.

She sat next to him and gently rested a hand on his knee, stroking the denim texture beneath her fingertips. Zachary stared ahead at the TV that wasn't on.

"What do you want me to do, Zach?" she asked softly. "I have to work. You know that."

He exhaled and shook his head. "I get that you have to work. I work too. The whole world works. But not everyone has a boss that clicks his fingers and makes his staff come running like drones!"

It was a fair point.

"Wait, you're not jealous of Josh, are you?" Keira asked. The thought was laughable. "If you only *saw* him!"

"Keira," Zachary barked, finally looking at her. "I'm not jealous of your boss. At least not in that way. I'm jealous that he gets so much of you, of your energy and your focus in life."

Now it was Keira's turn to sigh. She understood where Zach was coming from on one hand, but on the other she wished he could be supportive of her success. She wanted him to ride out this wave while she was at the bottom of the ladder. Things were about to get easier, once she'd made this next step in her career.

"I wish he didn't, either," Keira agreed. "But putting that much effort and energy into my career isn't going to change. At least not for the next month."

Zachary frowned. "What do you mean?"

Keira wanted to keep her excitement contained out of respect for Zach but she just couldn't help herself. She almost squealed as she said, "I'm going to Ireland!"

There was a long, long pause, as Zach absorbed the information.

"When?" he said, coolly.

"That's the thing," Keira replied. "It's a last-minute change of staff. Josh broke his leg. It's a whole long story."

Zach just glared as she rambled, looking at her expectantly for the punch line.

Keira hunkered down into the couch, trying to make herself seem as small as possible. "I leave tomorrow."

Zachary's expression turned as quickly as a flash storm. If he'd been rain clouds before, he was now thunder and lightning.

"But the wedding is tomorrow," he said.

Keira grabbed both his hands in hers. "The timing sucks, I'll be the first to admit it. But I swear Ruth won't mind."

"Won't mind?" Zach snapped, yanking his hands back. "You're in the wedding party!"

Suddenly he was on his feet, pacing away, running his hands through his hair. Keira leapt up and rushed to him, attempting to placate him with affection. But Zach was having none of it this time.

"I can't believe this," he gasped. "I spend all day hosting a brunch with *your* family, listening to Bryn going on and on about how hot her new meditation teacher is and all her vacuous opinions—"

"Hey!" Keira said, angry now. Criticizing her big sister was not okay.

"And instead of thanking me," Zach continued, "you drop this on me! How the hell am I supposed to tell Ruth?"

"I'll tell her," Keira suggested. "Let me be the bad guy, I don't mind."

"You are the bad guy!" Zach exclaimed.

He stomped out of the living room. Keira followed helplessly. They'd been together for two years and she'd never seen him this angry before.

11

She followed him into the bedroom and watched as he pulled her suitcase out from under the bed.

"What are you doing?" she asked, exasperated.

"Taking this out," he snapped back. "You can't go without a suitcase, can you?"

Keira shook her head. "I know you're angry but you're taking things a bit far."

She took the suitcase from his hands and slung it on the bed. It fell open as if inviting her to start packing it. Keira had to fight the urge inside of her to start filling it up.

Zach seemed to momentarily lose his strength. He deflated, sitting on the end of the bed with his head in his hands.

"You always choose work over me."

"I'm sorry," Keira said, not looking at him as she grabbed her favorite sweater from the floor and flung it discreetly into the case. "But this is an opportunity of a lifetime." She went over to the dresser and rummaged through her bottles of moisturizers and perfumes. "Ruth hates me anyway. She only put me in the bridal party because you asked her to."

"Because that's what you're supposed to do," Zach said sadly. "You're supposed to do family stuff together."

She turned and quickly added the items to her case. But Zach noticed what she was doing and his ever darkening expression grew darker still.

"Are you *packing*?"

Keira froze and chewed her bottom lip. "Sorry."

"No you're not," he said in a cold, measured way. Then he looked up and said, "If you go, I don't know if we can stay together."

Keira raised an eyebrow, nonplussed by his threat. "Oh really?" She folded her arms. Now he'd gotten her attention. "You're going to give me an ultimatum?"

Zachary threw his arms up in frustration. "Don't act like you're not forcing my hand! Can't you see how embarrassing it will be for me to turn up tomorrow at Ruth's wedding without you?"

Keira sighed, equally frustrated. "I don't understand why you can't just tell them that I've landed an awesome opportunity at work. Something that I couldn't miss."

"My sister's wedding should be something you can't miss. It should be a priority!"

Ah. There it was again. That word. Priority. The thing that Keira would never admit to Zach wasn't him but her career.

"I'm sorry," she repeated, feeling her resolve finally weaken. "But it's just not possible. My career has to come first."

She hung her head, not from shame but from sadness. It didn't have to be this way. Zach should never have pitted their relationship against her career. It was a battle he would inevitably lose.

Keira didn't know what else to say. She looked at Zachary's enraged face. No more words passed between them. There were none left to say. Then Zach got up from the bed, headed out of the room and down the corridor, and grabbed his keys from the bowl by the door before pulling the door open and slamming it shut behind him. As Keira listened to the sound of his car driving away, she knew he wouldn't be back tonight; he'd sleep on Ruth's fold-out couch to prove his point.

Keira had won the fight but there was no pleasure in her victory. She slumped onto the bed beside her open case and felt a hard lump form in her throat.

In need of some TLC, she grabbed her cell and called her mom.

"Hello, darling," the woman said, picking up right away, as if the sight of her youngest daughter's name on the caller ID had propelled her into immediate action. "Is everything okay?"

Keira sighed. "I was calling to tell you about an assignment I was given today at work. It's a cover story. I get to fly out to Ireland."

"Darling, that's wonderful news. How exciting! Congratulations. But why do you sound so glum?"

Keira rolled onto her stomach. "Zach. He's annoyed. He basically said if I went it would be over between us."

"I'm sure he doesn't mean it," her mom said kindly. "You know what men can be like. You've just bruised his ego by putting your own priorities above his."

Keira plucked the corner of a pillow case absentmindedly. "It's more to do with Ruth's wedding tomorrow," she explained. "He thinks I'm ditching him, leaving him in the lurch. Like if he turns up without a date his whole world will implode." She laughed wryly, but was met with silence on the other end of the line.

"Oh," her mother said.

"Oh what?" Keira asked, frowning.

Her mom's voice had lost some of its warmth. There was an edge to it that Keira recognized well enough, since she'd heard it a thousand times as a kid. Disapproval.

"Well, I didn't realize you'd be missing his sister's wedding," she said.

"And does that change things in your opinion?" Keira said, growing a little terse.

Her mom replied in the voice Keira recognized as "diplomatic." "If you had prior engagements already. And it is his sister. Turning up at weddings alone is really the worst. Everyone stares and whispers. He'll be quite uncomfortable."

"Mom!" Keira wailed. "This isn't the 1950s anymore. A man's comfort isn't more important than a woman's career!"

"That's not what I mean, darling," her mom said. "I just mean that Zachary is a lovely young man and there's nothing wrong with prioritizing the wedding. You don't want to be like your sister, always on those dating websites, having those terrible evenings with men who say they're six foot but then turn out to be barely five!"

"Mom!" Keira yelled again, cutting an end to her rambling. "I need you to be supportive right now."

Her mom sighed. "I am. I'm very pleased for you. And I love your … passion. I do."

Keira rolled her eyes. Her mom wasn't very good at being convincing.

"I just think that in this situation you should stay with your boyfriend. I mean, really, what matters more? You'll be quitting that job in three years anyway to start having babies."

"Okay, Mom, stop talking right now!" Keira snapped. Making babies was so far from her radar it was a laughable suggestion.

"Darling," her mom soothed. "It's very honorable that you work so hard. But love is important too. Just as important. If not more so. Does writing this article really mean more to you than Zachary?"

Keira realized she was gripping her phone tightly. She relaxed her grasp a little. "I have to go, Mom."

"Think about what I said."

"I will."

She hung up, her heart heavy. The elation she'd felt earlier today had entirely evaporated. There was only one person who could cheer her up now, and that was Bryn. She quickly found her big sister's contact details and called her.

"Hi, lil sis," Bryn said when she answered. "You missed brunch."

"I was working," Keira replied. "Joshua dragged us all into the office, I think just to show off in front of Elliot about this Ireland cover piece he was going to write. Only he slipped and… well, he broke his leg."

"Are you kidding?" Bryn exclaimed, bursting into hysterics. "How does that even happen?"

Already, Keira felt her unhappiness begin to melt away, such was the power of Bryn.

"It was insane," she said. "I saw his bone. And then he screamed about how he'd ruined his expensive pants!"

The two sisters laughed together.

"Then what happened?" Bryn asked, being the captive audience Keira had sought in Zachary and her mother.

"He was getting carried off on the gurney by the paramedics and I realized the meeting was about to start—Elliot hates it when people are late—so I went and sat down. And I guess I caught his eye because of that and he gave me the Ireland piece."

"No way!" Bryn exclaimed. "Are you kidding me? My baby sister is writing the cover story?"

Keira smiled. She knew Bryn didn't fully understand the extent to which this was a big deal for her, and was at least feigning twenty percent of her enthusiasm, but she appreciated it. It was the kind of reaction she'd hoped for from Zach.

"Yeah. It's great. But I have to go to Ireland tomorrow so I'm going to miss Ruth's wedding."

"Oh pft. So what?" Bryn said. "This is way more important. I didn't think you liked Ruth anyway."

"I don't. But I like *Zach*," Keira said, prompting Bryn to consider why jetting off to Ireland at the drop of a hat might not be the easiest thing to do in the world. "I've really upset him this time."

Bryn exhaled. "Look. Sis. I know this is hard. And I like the guy, believe me, I do. But you have got to go! You have to do this. I hate to be the one to say it but you really shouldn't be with a guy who holds you back. You'll only resent him if you give in to his demands."

"And he'll only resent me if I don't."

"Yup. It's a sad truth, but sometimes life just gets in the way of love. Two people can be right for each other but the timing can be all wrong."

Keira felt her chest ache at the thought of dumping Zachary in favor of her career. But maybe Bryn was right. Maybe it just wasn't the right time for them.

"So, what are you going to do?" Bryn asked, breaking Keira from her reverie.

Keira took a deep breath. "You know what, I've gone through too much crap climbing the corporate ladder to give up at the last hurdle. I *can't* turn this down."

Keira felt her drive return back to her. She was sad about the prospect of leaving Zachary behind, but she really didn't see any other option. Turning down this opportunity would be the end of her career. There were no two ways about it.

She had to go.

CHAPTER THREE

Keira's alarm clock woke her up at a stupidly early time the next morning, blaring like a foghorn. She rolled over and turned it off, then realized that the other side of the bed was empty. Zach hadn't slept there last night.

She got up, rubbing the sleep from her eyes, and peered into the living room. No Zach. So just as she'd predicted, he hadn't returned last night. He must have stayed at Ruth's.

Pushing her disappointment and sadness away, Keira took a quick shower, fighting hard to stop the warm water from lulling her back to sleep, and dressed in comfortable clothes for the long journey.

Grabbing her bag, she checked to make sure she had the tickets and itinerary that Heather had given her. Satisfied that her paperwork and passport were in her possession, she headed out of the house and hopped into the back of a waiting cab.

As she sped through the early morning streets of New York City, Keira took a moment to collect her frantic thoughts. This was really happening. She was really about to head abroad for work, something she'd always dreamed of doing. She just wished Zachary had chosen to share in this moment with her, rather than keep his distance.

The Newark airport was as busy as if it were rush hour on the subway. A 5 a.m. start was par for the course for so many busy career types, and Keira felt a sudden surge of pride to consider herself among them. She checked her luggage onto the flight, feeling like a superstar at LAX, her head held just as high. Then she found a coffee shop to get her morning fix and kill the time before her flight was ready to board.

As she sat in the bustling coffee shop, she checked her phone over and over. Even though she knew Zachary would still be sleeping, she desperately wanted some kind of communication from him. She knew she'd done the right thing by taking up the assignment and she hoped Zach would see it that way eventually. Or perhaps their relationship really was doomed like Bryn seemed to think it was. Perhaps their differing priorities really were a blockade they could no longer pass.

She fired off a light-hearted text to Zachary, leaving out any mention of their dispute, hoping that if he awoke to a sweet message he may feel more warmly toward her.

Her phone pinged and she leapt with excitement, thinking Zach had replied. But it was Heather checking everything had gone according to plan and she was on time for her flight. Disappointed, Keira texted back, telling Heather everything was fine.

Just then, she heard the boarding call for her flight. Quickly downing the last of her coffee, Keira headed to the check-in gate, vowing to call Zachary as soon as she landed. There was a five-hour time difference between New York and Ireland that she'd have to keep in mind throughout the duration of her stay.

On board the aircraft, Keira settled into her seat, checking one last time for any communication from Zach. But there was none, and the flight attendant flashed her a disapproving look to see her using her phone after they'd asked that all electronic devices be switched off. Sighing, Keira turned her phone off and stashed it in her pocket.

Just then, a crowd of stag party-goers crowded onto the flight, chatting loudly. Keira groaned. It was going to be a long flight. Seven hours, in fact, to Shannon in County Clare. It would be dark when she landed, but her body would think it was midday. She'd been hoping to get a bit of rest on the flight but the group of loud men was going to something of an impediment.

The plane began taxiing to the runway. In an attempt to block out the rowdy stag party, Keira put in earbuds and closed her eyes. But it wasn't anywhere near close enough to blocking out their loud banter.

The plane took to the air and Keira resigned herself to plan B: caffeine. She called over the air steward and ordered a coffee, knowing it would be the first of many. She drank it, huffily, to the background sound of the stag party.

As she cruised through the skies, Keira took some time to look through Heather's itinerary and reminders.

There aren't any cabs so a rental car will be waiting for you in the parking lot. I hope you can drive a stick shift. And remember to drive on the LEFT.

The thought of having to drive while so sleep deprived worried Keira. She hadn't driven in ages, since she usually took the subway everywhere. Stick shifts certainly presented an extra challenge. And driving on the left was going to be even harder. If she stood any chance of not crashing, she was going to need to drink a heck load more coffee!

You'll be staying at a traditional Irish pub and B&B so don't expect the Hilton treatment. It will be basic.

That didn't bother Keira. She'd been a starving writer ever since graduating from college; hotels had been out of her price range for years! She could slum it for a month no problem. As long as she wasn't expected to pee in an outhouse, she was certain she'd be able to survive even the most basic of accommodations.

You'll have the evening to acclimatize before work starts. We've arranged for a tour guide to show you around. You'll be meeting the matchmaker and festival owner the next morning. The festival begins the following evening.

Keira began to feel even more excited as she read through all the information. The flight seemed to be going by faster than she was expecting, which must have been thanks to the adrenaline pumping through her body. That and the copious amounts of caffeine.

Keira landed in Shannon in good spirits, stepping off the plane and into the cold, fresh September air. She'd been expecting to see rolling green hills and fields dotted with cows and sheep, but instead the Shannon airport wasn't much to look at. The area was somewhat industrialized, with large gray buildings that lacked any kind of architectural flare.

The car rental place was just as grim. Instead of a warm Irish greeting, she encountered a stony-faced young man who took her booking slip silently and handed her the keys without so much as uttering a syllable.

Keira took the keys and found the car in the lot. It was impossibly small. She got in the right-hand side, remembering Heather's reminder to drive on the left. It took her a while to refamiliarize herself with the concept of a stick shift and clutch pedal, and then she was off, using the SatNav to direct her out of Shannon. It would take approximately an hour to reach her destination, Lisdoonvarna.

No sooner had she left the main road than she found she was suddenly driving along small, winding roads with no sidewalks, no road signs, and no streetlights. Keira clutched the steering wheel anxiously and put every ounce of energy and concentration she had into driving along the roads that just seemed to become narrower and narrower.

After fifteen minutes or so, she began to relax somewhat. The traffic was very light, which helped calm her nerves because she wasn't so terrified about crashing into anyone. The environment was also very relaxing, with nothing around for miles but hillsides and fields dotted with sheep. The grass was the greenest green Keira had ever seen in her life. She wound down the window in order to sniff the pure air, but instead got the smell of manure. She wound the window up quickly.

There were hardly any roads signs to guide her so she was thankful for the SatNav. But there were also no streetlights, which made driving difficult, especially with so many tight, blind corners. And the markings on the road had all but faded. Keira also found driving on the left disorientating. The difficult drive was compounded further by the sheer number of tractors she had to overtake!

Just then the road became so narrow there was only space for one car. Keira almost plowed headlong into oncoming traffic and had to squeal to a halt, the car juddering to the side of the road and scraping against the hedgerow. Keira held a hand up to apologize to the driver of the other car but they just smiled kindly as if it were no bother at all, and reversed a little in order to allow the space for her to pass. Back home in New York City, such an incident would have resulted in Keira being loudly cussed. She was already getting a feel for that infamous Irish hospitality.

Her heart still pounding from the shock of the near miss, Keira managed to slowly inch forward past the car.

She continued onward cautiously, feeling more terrified of the roads than she had before. She hoped the scrape against the hedges wouldn't be visible on the paint work—she wasn't sure how the company would feel about her coming back with a huge bill from the car rental place for damage!

Any residue of excitement she'd been feeling before the treacherous drive had begun started to wane. Running on adrenaline and coffee had only gotten Keira so far. Now instead of being in awe of the beauty of nature, she saw her surroundings as sparse and somewhat bleak. The only living creatures she saw were sheep. There were old stone farmhouses dotted around that were abandoned, crumbling. Up in the hillsides, Keira also saw a derelict castle nestled within a smattering of trees and wondered how such a historic old building had been left to decay.

She began mentally taking notes for her article, remembering the cynical angle Elliot wanted her to take. Instead of seeing the beauty in the coastal view, she focused instead on the gray clouds. Instead of seeing the vast view over the ocean as miraculous, she instead decided to cast her gaze to the bleakness of the distant craggy mountains. Though it was stunningly beautiful on one hand, Keira felt that debunking the romance of Ireland wouldn't be that much of a challenge. She just needed to know where to look and how to twist things.

She passed through a handful of small, stone-walled towns. One was called Killinaboy and she laughed aloud, quickly texting a picture of the town sign to Zach, who she hoped would appreciate it.

She was so distracted by the amusing road sign, Keira almost didn't notice the next obstacle in the road—a herd of sheep! She slammed on the brakes and came to a halt just in time, stalling the car in the process. It took a long time for her terror to abate. She could have mown down a whole family of sheep!

Taking a moment to calm her heartbeat, Keira grabbed her phone and took a photo of the crowd of sheep's backsides, sending it to Zach with the caption: *the traffic here is a nightmare.*

Of course, she received no reply. Frustrated with his complete lack of interest, she sent the same pictures off to Nina and Bryn in turn. Both responded almost immediately with laughing emojis and Keira nodded, satisfied to know that at least someone in her life found her escapades interesting.

Keira revved the engine back to life and slowly overtook the convoy of sheep. They watched her pass with knowing expressions and she almost found herself apologizing aloud. The sky was starting to darken, making the drive feel even more precarious. It didn't help that the only buildings she saw were churches, with solemn statues of the Virgin Mary praying by the roadsides.

Finally, Keira arrived in Lisdoonvarna and was pleasantly surprised by what she saw. At least it looked like a place where people lived! There were streets where more than one house stood side by side, which gave it the feel of a town… almost. All the buildings, houses, and shops were so small and quaint, many barely a couple of feet away from the road, and they were painted in bright rainbow colors. Keira was glad to finally be somewhere that seemed like a community rather than just single dwellings connected by roads.

She slowed her car, following the street signs until she found the address she was looking for, the St. Paddy's Inn. The B&B was right on the corner of two roads, a three-story, dark red brick building. From the outside, it looked very Irish to Keira.

She parked in the small lot and leapt out, grabbing her bags from the trunk. She was exhausted and ready to get inside and rest.

But as she approached, she realized rest was not something she was about to get. Because even from here she could hear the sounds of merry conversation and rowdy debate. She could also hear the sound of live music, of violins, pianos, and accordions.

A bell over the door tinkled as she walked inside to find a small, dark pub with old crimson wallpaper and several round wooden tables. The place was filled to the brim with people, beers in hand. They looked over at her as if they could tell right away she didn't belong here, that she wasn't just a tourist, but an American.

Keira felt a little overwhelmed by the culture shock.

"What can I get yee?" a male voice said in a thick accent that Keira could hardly understand.

She turned to the bar to see an old man standing behind it. He had a wizened face and a tuft of gray hair sprouting from the center of an otherwise bald head.

"I'm Keira Swanson," Keira said, approaching him. "From *Viatorum* magazine."

"I can't hear yee! Speak up!"

Keira raised her voice over the live folk music and repeated her name. "I have a room booked here," she added when the man just looked at her with a blank frown. "I'm a writer from America."

At last the man seemed to understand who she was and why she was there.

"Of course!" he exclaimed, a smile spreading across his face. "From the paper with the fancy Latin name."

He had a warm aura about him, very grandfatherly, and Keira felt herself relax again.

"That's the one," she confirmed.

"I'm Orin," he said. "I own the St. Paddy. Live here too. And this is for you." Suddenly, a pint of Guinness was plonked onto the bar in front of Keira. "A traditional St. Paddy welcome."

Keira was taken aback. "I'm not much of a drinker," she laughed.

Orin gave her a look. "You are while you're in County Clare, my lass! You're here to let your hair down just like the rest of the locals. And anyway, we have to toast your safe journey! Thanks be to the Virgin Mary." He crossed his chest.

Keira felt a bit shy as she accepted the Guinness and took a sip of the strong, creamy liquid. She'd never tasted Guinness before and the flavor wasn't particularly agreeable to her. After just one sip she was certain she wouldn't be able to finish the entire pint.

"Everyone," Orin called out to the patrons in the pub, "this is the American reporter!"

Keira cringed as the whole pub turned around and began clapping and cheering like she was some kind of celebrity.

"We're so excited you're here!" a woman with frizzy hair said, leaning in a little too close and smiling a little too widely for

22

Keira's comfort. Then in a lower voice she added, "You might want to wipe off your Guinness stash."

Feeling her cheeks burn with embarrassment, Keira quickly wiped the suds from her top lip. A second later, another of the pub's patrons had wedged her way forward, barging elbows with others on her way—not that anyone seemed to mind. Her drink spilled a little as she stumbled. "I can't wait to read your piece!"

"Oh, thanks," Keira said, shrugging. It hadn't occurred to her that the people here would want to read what she'd written about them. It might make the whole cynical angle a little harder for her to pull off.

"So what made you want to be a reporter?" the man next to her said.

"I'm just a writer," Keira said with a blush, "not a reporter."

"Just a writer?" the man exclaimed, speaking loudly and looking for the attention of the others around him. "You hear that? She says she's *just* a writer. Well, I can barely hold a pen so you're a genius as far as I'm concerned."

Everyone laughed. Keira nervously drank small sips of her Guinness. The Irish hospitality was very welcome but it was also a culture shock, and she found herself cringing, thinking of the myriad ways she could bash this place in her piece.

"I'll show you to your room," Orin said finally, once she'd managed to drink almost half the pint of Guinness.

She followed him up a creaking, narrow stairway and along a corridor with a threadbare carpet that smelled strongly of dust. Keira walked silently, taking it all in, constructing cutting sentences in her head as she observed the dated decor. The walls were decorated with framed, faded photographs of local soccer teams from the past and Keira smirked when she saw that the majority of the players shared the same surname, O'Sullivan. She took a discreet picture of the black-and-white soccer team and pinged it off to Zach with the caption: *Mr. O'Sullivan must have been a prolific breeder.*

"Here you go," Orin said, opening a door and showing her inside.

The room was awful. Though large, with a double bed and a huge window, it was decorated horribly. The wallpaper was a sort of peach color, stained in places as if from years of grubby handprints. The bed had a thin duvet on it, which was quilted but not in an endearing country-house way, more in a thrift store castaway way.

"This is the room with the desk," Orin said, grinning with pride, gesturing to a small wooden desk under the window. "For your writing."

Keira blushed. She was inwardly horrified at the thought of staying in the grimy room for an entire month, but she managed to squeeze out a grateful, "Thank you." So much for thinking she'd be able to slum it for a month!

"Do you want a bit of time to settle in before meeting Shane?" Orin asked.

Keira frowned, confused. "Who's Shane?"

"Shane Lawder. Your tour guide. For the festival," Orin explained.

"Of course," Keira said, remembering in Heather's notes she'd said there would be a tour guide. "Yes, please, I'd like to meet Shane." She had no desire to spend another minute in the room, so she dumped her bag on the bed and headed back down the creaking staircase.

"Shane!" Orin cried as he took his position back behind the bar.

To Keira's surprise, it was the fiddle player who responded. He put his instrument down—though the group of musicians he was playing with carried on as if nothing had happened at all—and came over.

Beneath his scraggly beard, Keira could tell he had a chiseled jawline. In fact, if it weren't for his hair, which desperately needed cutting, and scruffy clothing, Shane would be quite handsome. Keira felt guilty for thinking such a thing, especially since things with Zach were on such rocky ground at the moment, but she thought of Bryn's motto: *Ain't nothing wrong with looking.*

"You don't look much like a Joshua," Shane said as he shook her hand.

"Oh, didn't anyone tell you?" Keira said. "Something came up so I was sent instead. Sorry about that."

Shane gave her a cheeky look. "What are you apologizing about? I'd much prefer to spend thirty days with a fine-looking lady like you. No offense to this Joshua fellow, I'm sure he's attractive enough, but he doesn't sound like my type. You know, being male and all."

Keira gulped. She hadn't expected Irish men to be quite so forward. But she reminded herself of Zach and repeated the mantra in her head that she was just looking.

As Shane took a barstool beside her, Orin put a Guinness in front of each of them. Keira groaned silently. She couldn't handle this much alcohol!

Shane took a deep sip of his drink, then spread some documents onto the bar.

"The Festival of Love is thirty days long," he explained. "Most of the activities don't start until the evenings so I've prepared an itinerary of places we can visit while you're here, so you can get a better feel of the country as a whole. We'll start with the Burren for the mountain scenes, then the Cliffs of Moher to look at the ocean, then we'll head over to the next county, Kerry, to the beautiful old stately home in Killarney, then onwards to Dingle."

"I thought you were just guiding me through the festival," Keira said. "Not the whole country!"

"You'll go crazy if you don't get a bit of space from Lisdoonvarna during the day," Shane explained. "The sheer amount of groups of people coming and going, it gets a little much."

Keira laughed silently to herself. She seriously doubted Lisdoonvarna was anywhere near as hectic during the festival as New York City was on any normal day.

"There's a lot of drinking," Shane continued. "Some of the parties go on until the early hours of the next day. I say some, but really it's most."

Keira thought of the rowdy stag party she'd shared the flight over with and wondered whether she was going to get any sleep over the next month at all.

"This looks great," she said, glancing over the itinerary. "But I will need some time each day to write. It can't be all fun and games."

Shane smirked at her. "You only just got here and you're already thinking about work?"

"I have to," Keira explained. "This is a really big deal for me. I don't want to screw it up."

"And not screwing it up equates to not letting your hair down?"

Keira wasn't in the mood to be challenged about her life choices. She'd had just about as much of that as she cared for from Zach and her mom.

"It just means setting aside time each day to write," she refuted, sounded a little huffy.

Shane's expression remained in an amused kind of smirk. He took a languorous swig from his pint. "You're one of those straight-laced types, aren't you?" he quipped. "All work and no play."

Keira gave him an unimpressed look. "I don't know how you can presume to know anything about me," she said. "You've known me for all of five minutes."

Shane just kept smirking. He didn't reply, as though the argument was already settled.

Keira tensed up. He was handsome, that was true, but if he carried on like this he was going to get on her nerves. She didn't know if she could handle thirty days of teasing and drinking and not getting any space to write.

Maybe this assignment was going to be harder than she'd expected.

*

Keira finally managed to excuse herself at midnight. She'd lost count of the number of Guinnesses Orin and Shane had sunk, but luckily for her they'd stopped cajoling her to keep up with them. Still, her head was spinning somewhat as she climbed the stairs to her room.

She shut the door, but the pounding sound of the music and merriment downstairs didn't cease. Keira felt fraught, like she was wound far too tightly. She checked her phone, but found that there was no message from Zach. He would definitely have had the time to read them by now. Which meant he was giving her the silent treatment. *How mature,* Keira thought.

At least she'd received responses from both Nina and Bryn, asking a myriad of questions. She texted Nina—who would be editing the piece—to tell her that her itinerary was filled to the brim and not to expect any work for a while. To Bryn, she texted a brief description of Shane's physical features and some flame emojis.

He's a pain, though. One of those arrogant guys who thinks it's endearing to tease you.

Bryn's reply came quickly. *It IS endearing.*

Keira laughed and put her phone away. The music downstairs was certainly going to keep her awake for some hours, so she may as well put in some time on her laptop. She took it from her bag and began writing an email to Elliot with some of her initial ideas for approaching the article. Thanks to all the Guinnesses, she found herself able to adopt an even snarkier tone that she'd anticipated.

If you've ever wondered what decades' worth of stale Guinness smooshed into a carpet smells like, then look no further than St. Paddy's Inn in Lisdoonvarna, County Clare. As an exotic American, my arrival here prompted an outpouring of suffocating Irish hospitality. I say suffocating, because turning down the offers of copious amounts of alcohol was simply not an option, hence the aforementioned stale Guinness smell that permeates every inch of this gritty, dark dive. In fact, the place is so saturated with Guinness the carpets, curtains, and wallpaper are all tacky to the touch. Let's just say I won't be surprised if the water of my morning shower (in the dated, cramped en suite) comes out black and frothy...

She continued in the same snarky tone. She knew it was mean to bash the B&B and the friendly people she had thus far met but she just couldn't help herself.

She finished up and hit send. Elliot replied almost immediately with a praising email.

Keep this up, Keira. It's gold!

Just then, Keira's phone rang. It was Bryn. Keira sighed, realizing she wasn't going to get any more work done tonight. She folded down her laptop and answered the call, climbing into bed as she did so.

"What's up?" she asked her sister.

"I just had a failure of a date," Bryn explained. "So I thought I'd call you for the lowdown on this hunky tour guide."

Keira laughed. "Well, he has too much hair. And his fashion sense sucks. But he would scrub up nicely."

"I think you should go for it," Bryn said.

Keira gasped, surprised by how forward Bryn was being, even for her. "What about Zach!" she laughed.

"What about him?" Bryn replied dismissively.

Keira groaned. "He's my *boyfriend,*" she reminded Bryn. "And even if Shane got a haircut and a whole new wardrobe I wouldn't be able to spend more than five minutes in his company before throttling him."

Bryn laughed. "That's going to make the next few weeks a bit difficult, isn't it?"

"That and the fact that my room is above a pub that seems to have no closing time and a live folk band twenty-four/seven."

"That sounds amazing," Bryn refuted. "Jeez, Keira, you work so hard you can't even see what an exciting situation you're in! You've just told me the party never stops with a *groan.*"

"You sound like Shane," Keira replied. "If I don't want to drink, dance, and be merry I don't have to!"

She and Bryn finished up their conversation, and Keira found that in spite of all the noise coming from downstairs, she was hardly able to keep her eyes open. So she settled down under the thin cover and rested her head against the lumpy pillow. There was still no response from Zach to any of her humorous texts. She tried calling him but the phone just rang and rang.

She checked Instagram and saw photos of Zach at Ruth's wedding. He was looking gorgeous in his suit, but his expression was so lonely. He seemed awkward standing there alone, and she felt bad not to be there with him. Maybe her mom had had a slight point. Turning up at weddings alone clearly was very embarrassing.

As she began to fall into slumber, Keira began dreaming that she was there at the wedding with Zach. Only it wasn't Zach, it was Shane, shaved and in a sharp suit. He looked more handsome than she'd even anticipated.

Keira woke herself with a start. Things were already complicated enough without her developing a crush on her tour guide!

She pushed all the thoughts from her mind and, finally, fell into a deep sleep.

CHAPTER FOUR

"Did you sleep well?" Orin asked the second Keira descended the staircase early the next morning, emerging into the pub part of the B&B.

She rubbed her bleary eyes. "Yes, thanks." The lie came so easily. Much better to pretend she loved her rickety bed, thin duvet, and lumpy pillows than to complain and have Orin fuss about it. She could write about it later, after all, and get some cathartic release that way.

"Take a seat and have some breakfast," Orin said, leading her to a table and placing a coffee in front of her. It was swiftly followed by a bowl of oatmeal. He sat in the seat opposite. "I've made it the Irish way. I hope you like it."

He was grinning rather widely.

"What's the Irish way?" Keira murmured suspiciously.

She took a sip of the coffee and was surprised by how delicious it tasted. Whatever the Irish way was, it was good! Then she spooned some of her oatmeal into her mouth and almost cried out in delight. She'd never tasted anything so creamy, so utterly fantastic.

"Wow, what makes this taste so great?" Keira said, as she munched on another spoon of oatmeal. "Are the cows fed organic grass and milked by the hands of maidens?" she joked.

Orin's grin grew wider. "Baileys in the coffee. And a splash of whiskey in the milk."

Keira was shocked. "Liquor at eight a.m.?" she gasped. "Is that a good idea?"

Orin gave her a wink. "The best way to start the day. That and a brisk walk. Which you'll get just as soon as I escort you to your meeting with William Barry, the head of the festival."

Keira realized then that Orin was already ready to leave the B&B. He was wearing boots that reached halfway up his calves as if in anticipation of puddles. Or mud. Either way, Keira wasn't in the mood for perambulating.

"You don't have to do that," she said. "I have SatNav in the car so I won't get lost."

Orin pointed at her coffee. "That's not why I'm doing it."

The cynical part of Keira's mind wondered whether Orin had deliberately inebriated her in order to ensure she couldn't refuse his offer of a walk. But she knew that was crazy thinking. Orin was just a gentle old man, proud of his town. He wanted to show it off to the cynical New Yorker he'd been lumped with.

29

"Come on," Orin continued. "You're here to get a real taste of Ireland! To live like a local! You won't really know what our lives are like if you don't walk a mile in our shoes!"

He yanked on her arm playfully, encouraging her to join him. His enthusiasm was quickly turning to cajoling and Keira realized there was literally no way of turning him down. Orin was going to make her walk to the meeting with him no matter what she said! There was no refusing.

Giving in, she downed the last of her boozy coffee, feeling the effects as soon as she stood. Then she and Orin left the dark B&B and emerged into the bright early morning sunshine. Even though the sky was a muted gray, Keira squinted against its harsh glare.

"Lead the way," she said to Orin, as she glanced down the only path, a winding country road that snaked its way down the hillside. There were occasional buildings dotted on either side but it was mainly surrounded by lush green fields filled with sheep.

"It's a two-mile walk to the town hall if we stick to the road," Orin said. "But if we cut across the fields it's half that distance. Of course, the farmer has every right to shoot us since we'd be trespassing but everyone around here knows everyone else so we'll be fine."

Keira gulped. "Let's take the scenic route, huh?" she said.

"If you want," Orin said nonchalantly, clearly not even picking up on her alarm.

They began strolling down the street. Despite the early hour, everyone they passed seemed so happy and friendly. When they reached the main street (if it could be called such) there was even a small troupe of musicians playing fiddles and accordions, singing old folk songs. People danced and sang along. Keira couldn't really believe what she was seeing. How could a place be so collectively happy? Maybe she'd been wrong to make such harsh, snap judgments.

"Here we go," Orin said as they arrived at their destination.

Like all the buildings in Lisdoonvarna this one was brightly painted, a burnt orange color in this case, adding to the rainbow streets. A sign above the door proclaimed: Home of the Matchmaker. The door itself was covered in images of cupid.

Keira raised an eyebrow at the tacky decor, then followed Orin inside. An elderly gentleman rose from his desk and came toward her.

"William Barry," he said, extending a hand. "You're the American reporter."

Keira shook his hand. "I'm a travel writer, not a reporter."

"So this piece isn't going in the *New York Times*?" William asked, frowning.

Keira glanced appealingly at Orin. Had William been under the impression she worked for some huge organization? What if Heather had bent the truth a little as she'd organized this event, knowing that Josh would have been willing to lie and sweet talk his way to his goal?

Suddenly, Orin burst out laughing. Keira looked back at William. He was creased over with laughter as well.

"You should have seen the look on your face!" he exclaimed, his face turning bright red.

Keira wasn't quite able to see the funny side. There was too much at stake for her with her first real assignment that teasing was not exactly welcome.

"Take a seat, take a seat," William said as his laughter began subsiding.

Keira did, drawing up one of the wooden chairs and sitting at the desk. Orin sat beside her. Just as William sat down, a woman with fiery red hair entered holding a tray with a teapot, mugs, and a milk jug on it.

"This is my secretary, Maeve," William said as the woman put the tray down. "Thanks, dear."

She disappeared out of the room, leaving William to pour the cups of tea. It didn't matter that Keira wasn't much of a tea drinker, she felt unable to decline, and so she took the mug of steaming tea without protest.

William folded his hands across the table. "I must say we're ever so excited to have you here, Keira. With the way the world is changing and all these Internet dating sites, it's becoming harder and harder to get customers. I'm hoping your piece ignites some renewed interest."

Keira covered her guilty expression with her tea mug. She felt bad knowing that she was going to write such a cutting piece. William and Orin seemed like sweet, genuine people, and they'd treated her with such hospitality. But she had her assignment, had her instructions. She told herself that bashing a silly festival from halfway around the globe in a magazine that didn't even get imported to Ireland would hardly cause their business to fold.

"Do you know the history of the festival?" William continued.

"I did some research before I came," Keira said, nodding.

But as William launched into his monologue about the festival, she shut her mouth. Clearly she was going to be given the aural history whether she liked it or not.

"It was my father's business. His father's before that. In fact, the Barrys have been matchmakers for as long as anyone can remember. Way back then it was about matching the nobles who were visiting for the water with a beautiful young local girl. Irish girls are considered very prolific child bearers, you see, which was a matchmaker's main selling point."

Keira could hardly stop the look of disgust on her face. William didn't notice, however, and continued with his story.

"It would usually take place just after the harvest, when the girls were at their plumpest and their bosoms fullest. A good matchmaker would make sure the girls were married and whisked away before winter fell, since the chances were they'd get pneumonia and die over the winter."

Keira pressed her lips together to stifle a giggle. She couldn't tell how much of what William said was tongue in cheek but she had a slight inkling that he was deadly serious. Though she'd done her research, hearing the way William phrased it really was amusing.

"Then of course times changed. Different sorts came to the town. Wars depleted the male stock. The threat of famine made people desperate to marry young, and marry anyone. It was a hard time for the matchmaker. When I took over the business from my pa I was mainly paid by farm apprentices to match them with one of my local girls." He patted a book. "So I kept a list of them."

"Is that legal?" Keira said, finally breaking her stunned silence. "It sounds a bit stalkerish to me."

"Nonsense!" William laughed. "The girls loved it. They all want to get married. Even if it is to a farm hand with no brain cells to his name and terrible hygiene habits."

Keira just shook her head. Her article was writing itself!

Just then, the door opened. Keira was expecting to see the flame-haired Maeve again, but when she looked over her shoulder it was Shane she saw entering the building. She suddenly felt tingly all over and sat up, stiff-backed, in her chair.

"Morning," Shane said, taking a seat in the corner.

William continued. "Now here is my book of matches." He handed her a huge, hardback leather tome. "Well, one of them. I've been doing this for so many years now I've got quite the collection."

Keira began to thumb through the book, reading all the names of happy couples. Some included photos, others had dates of weddings. There were cards addressed to William from couples he

32

had matched. It all looked very twee. Keira, ever calculating, began to formulate a paragraph for her article in her mind.

"You know," William said, leaning across the table toward her. "I could match you. Maybe a nice Irish lad is just what you need."

Keira felt her cheeks burn. "I have a boyfriend," she said. Maybe she imagined it, but out of the corner of her eye, she thought she saw Shane flinch. "Zach. He works in computers."

"You're happy with this man?" William asked.

"Yes, very," Keira replied, trotting out the old party line.

William didn't look convinced. He tapped the book that Keira had set down on the desk. "I've been doing this a long time. I'm an expert in love and I can see it in people's eyes. I'm not so certain this man is right for you."

Keira knew he wasn't trying to be rude, but his skepticism touched a nerve, especially with her and Zach arguing so much at the moment. But William was also journalism gold and she wanted as much out of him as possible.

"Not right for me in what way?" she pressed.

"He doesn't support you in the ways you need. You're no longer growing together, no longer following the same path."

Keira felt chills all over. This was far too close to the bone.

"You're a fortune teller as well as a matchmaker?" she quipped. "You hiding a bunch of tarot cards under there?"

William let out a belly laugh. "Oh no, nothing like that. But I have developed an intuition over the years. There was no sparkle in your eyes when you said his name. No lilt in your voice."

"I think that's just my cynical New Yorker personality," Keira said.

"Maybe. Or maybe it's because you don't really love him."

Keira pondered that statement. She and Zach rarely exchanged the L word. In fact, she couldn't even recall when they last had.

"I don't think love always has to come into these things," she said.

"But why waste your time with someone you don't love when you could be out looking for The One?"

Keira folded her arms. "Because maybe there isn't a 'One.'"

"You don't believe in The One?" William pressed.

Keira shook her head. "Nope."

This admission seemed to excite William. "We have a naysayer," he exclaimed with a laugh. "Which means it's our challenge to change your mind. Shane, lad?" He gestured for the tour guide to come over, which he did. Once he was standing beside him, William slung an arm across his shoulders. "You've been promoted," he joked. "You're no longer just to guide this young woman through the festival, you're to guide her towards true love. I fear it may be a tall order!"

Keira shuffled uncomfortably in her seat. But despite her discomfort at being the center of the strange meeting, she knew she'd collected some excellent material for her article, thanks to the doddering old man and his antiquated opinions on relationships. Elliot was going to love this. And writing it, for Keira, would be somewhat therapeutic.

She just had to get through her first day with Shane and then she'd be able to purge herself of all this silliness by typing.

CHAPTER FIVE

"I don't know how long this trip we're going on is supposed to be," Keira said as she got into the passenger side of Shane's car and fiddled with her seat belt. "But I need a coffee ASAP. And if you could get me back with a few hours to spare before the festival kicks off that would be great. I need to get in some solid writing hours." She finally got buckled in. "So, where are we going?"

When she received no response from Shane she looked over to see him wearing his characteristic amused expression. She folded her arms. "What?"

He gave her a shrug. "Well, it's hardly the weather for sunglasses, that's all I was thinking."

Keira pushed her sunglasses resolutely against her nose. "There might be early morning glare," she replied, cringing at the haughtiness she heard in her voice. "And anyway, you're hardly one to judge someone else's attire. Did you even use a mirror to dress this morning?"

Shane tipped his head back and laughed with abandon. Keira felt her lips twitch with satisfaction, then checked herself. She'd just allowed herself to take one step closer toward flirting with him, which definitely was not part of the *ain't nothing wrong with looking* philosophy!

"I thought I would take you somewhere nearby to start off with," Shane told her as he accelerated onto the main street. "So I've chosen the Burren, which is only a twenty-minute drive. It's a national park. You heard of it?"

Keira shook her head. "I can't wait," she said as a mental picture formulated in her mind of a beautiful Irish scene.

She wasn't sure, but she thought she saw Shane smirk. When they pulled up in the parking lot of the Burren twenty minutes later she realized why. There wasn't a blade of grass in sight! The Burren was made of bleak, gray rock.

She turned to Shane, frowning. "Is this a prank? I thought you said it was a national park."

Shane started laughing. "It is! One and a half thousand hectares of protected land, consisting almost entirely of limestone."

Keira let out a sigh of exasperation. "So of all the places you could have taken me to show off the majesty of Ireland, you chose this."

"I picked up on some snooty vibes back at William's place," Shane said, raising a combative eyebrow. "I figured this would be the best place to take you to get you off your high horse. Ireland

35

isn't some fantasy land filled with leprechauns, though there are some parts that play up the stereotypes for the sake of the tourists. But if you dig a little bit beneath the surface we're a country with real heart, real romance. We have a rich and interesting history, if you let yourself give us a chance."

Keira folded her arms. Everything he'd said about her was right, of course, but she wasn't about to admit that. "I'm not snooty," was all she said.

Shane just shrugged. "Come on, this way. The view from the top of the hill is incredible."

Keira followed. "I don't really have the appropriate footwear for a hike," she complained.

"Don't worry, I won't take us on the three-hour mountain trek, although it's breathtaking and a shame to miss out on." He gave her a withering look. "Think you can handle a half hour loop? It'll take us through meadows and some amazing woodland."

"Yes, I think I can I manage thirty minutes," Keira muttered.

"I meant without killing me," Shane laughed.

He seemed to enjoy winding Keira up.

"I feel like we've gotten off to a bad start," Keira said as she tried to keep up with his brisk pace. She wasn't used to hilly walks. "Have I said something to insult you?"

At first, Shane ignored the question. Instead, he pointed to a wooden stake in the ground with several colorful arrows on it. "We're following the orange trail, okay?"

Keira nodded. They continued ascending the gray hillside. The landscape was so barren Keira felt as if she were walking on the surface of the moon. The craggy craters on either side of her added further to the illusion. When she saw a tuft of grass—somehow growing through a crack in the rock—it gave her a bit of a shock to think that grass could grow on the moon. She had to remind herself that this place was actually on Earth.

"Well?" Keira pressed. "You didn't answer my question."

"About whether we got off on the wrong foot or not?" Shane said. Then he chewed his bottom lip in contemplation. "Why does it matter?"

"Because we have thirty days to spend together so we may as well get along."

Shane fell silent again. Keira couldn't help but feel frustrated by the amount of time it took him to answer a question. She wasn't comfortable with the silences he was constantly bestowing on her. It made her feel awkward.

"I wonder," he said finally, "if you just don't like the idea that someone might not like you."

"Excuse me?" Keira felt instantly insulted by his comment and immediately put up a defensive front.

"You have one of those nice-guy complexes. You expect everyone to find your quirky Americanness charming and I don't."

"*Me* charming?" Keira scoffed. "You're the one with the whole cheeky Irish chappy thing going on!"

"That bothers you?"

"It's an infuriating stereotype."

Keira could hear herself growing snappy. In complete contrast, Shane's tone hadn't changed at all. He was completely neutral, as though the conversation wasn't even remotely irksome.

"I think you're finding a lot more than just me infuriating," Shane said. "I mean, you weren't that nice to William."

"And?" Keira scoffed. "I'm here to work, not make friends. And I feel no obligation to be nice to someone with such old-fashioned ideas about love. It annoys me when people think they know exactly what men and women want from one another."

Shane raised his eyebrows. "For someone who says they're happy in their long-term relationship you seem very hostile towards the concept of love."

Keira shot him a look. "It's not love that's the problem. It's this idea that it's a picture-perfect thing. That some old man who's never met you in your life can just match you to someone else he doesn't know from Adam, and then you'll fall instantly in love and stay that way forever and ever. Real life isn't like a novel."

Even as she spoke, Keira could tell that Shane was enjoying her reaction. He was deliberately winding her up. *Two can play that game,* Keira thought.

"So you're a romantic then?" she said. "Is that what you're telling me? I suppose you've only ever been with your high school sweetheart and plan on marrying her."

Suddenly, Shane fell silent, and Keira could tell she'd accidentally spoken out of turn. She snapped her lips shut, knowing not to press it any further.

They reached the top of the hill and an incredible view opened up before Keira. It was like looking at the cooled lava of a volcano, or the surface of an asteroid. Keira had never seen anything quite like this alien landscape, and never had she felt so small or insignificant.

For the first time since arriving, Keira felt a new sense of humbleness. Maybe Elliot *had* made a mistake sending her to

Ireland. Joshua would never have come over all sentimental at the sight of a beautiful, mystical landscape. He'd remain cynical and cold just like Elliot needed him to be. But Keira herself could feel something in her core softening. For the first time since arriving in Ireland she felt as though something in its bleak barrenness had touched her.

"Come on," Shane said, his voice lacking all of the joviality she'd become accustomed to. "Let's go."

"Can we stay a bit longer?" Keira asked.

"I thought you needed a coffee."

"It can wait."

They stood side by side, silent, watching the world. There was no one around for miles, not another living soul. Keira couldn't recall any other point in her life when she'd been in such a remote location. Back home in New York City she was always surrounded by people, by noise and civilization. But here there was just nature in its starkest form.

"Did I say something to upset you?" Keira asked Shane.

It had been a good ten minutes since he'd uttered a word. It felt so strange to not hear him taking a swipe at her.

"Actually, yes," Shane said finally.

"Oh." Keira hadn't been expecting such candor. In some ways it was refreshing. But the brutal truth could be just that: brutal. "I'm sorry for whatever it was I said."

Shane looked at her for the first time in a long time. "I'm not sure you are."

He began walking again, descending now, leaving Keira standing, floundering on the precipice of the world. She finally pulled herself together and followed.

"That's not fair," she said, stepping up beside him, swinging her arms in wide arcs in order to keep up.

"Oh?" was all Shane deigned to give her.

Keira felt that now familiar sense of irritation. "You can't accuse me of not being sorry."

"Well, you don't know what you need to be sorry for," Shane replied. "So how can you know if you're sorry about it?"

Keira frowned. Shane was talking in riddles again. "I can know I'm sorry for hurting your feelings even if I don't know how I did it!"

Shane shrugged. "Maybe."

"What's that supposed to mean?" Keira challenged. Then in her best Irish accent, she mimicked, "Maybe."

Shane burst out laughing. "Wow. I knew Americans were bad at accents but that was exceptional. You could win an award for that."

Keira let out a frustrated exhalation. At least Shane was back on form. Back to his predictably irritating state.

They reached the car. Keira could feel the warmth in her cheeks. Her breath came in short puffs.

"You're not very fit, are you?" Shane joked as he opened the passenger door for her.

"I'm just not used to hills," Keira replied testily. "But let me guess, you're some kind of Olympic hiker?"

Shane let out one of his deep laughs and Keira felt a tingle inside of her; she liked making Shane laugh like that, it made her feel good about herself, confident.

"Olympic hiking, now that's an idea," Shane said, shaking his head. "No, not quite. But my dad taught me how to box. And I grew up beside a lake so I'm not too shabby at swimming, either."

As she got into the car, Keira pretended to be unimpressed, but a mental picture had formed in her head of Shane's muscular body emerging from a lake, his boxer's biceps glistening with water. It was hard to imagine a firm, muscled body existing beneath his ill-fitting shirt and jeans combo, but now that Keira had done so she couldn't seem to shake it.

Shane came and sat in the driver's seat beside her. Keira was never going to get over how small the cars were over here, and how close it made her feel to whoever was in the car with her.

"So you're strong?" she said, noting the completely unintentional flirtatious lilt in her voice that she hoped wasn't too pronounced.

She half expected Shane to pull up his sleeve and flex, but instead he just gave one of his nonchalant shrugs. "You could say that."

He gunned the engine and reversed them out of the Burren's parking lot. Keira gave it a long, wistful look as they drove away, knowing that she'd experienced something profound there, something that would stay with her forever.

*

They returned to find Lisdoonvarna festival in full swing. The streets teemed with men and women alike, all dressed up to the nines. Shops and bars had opened their doors and turned on their lights, making the town a disco ball of color. Everywhere Keira

39

looked there was another musician, another band surrounded by a crowd of people singing and dancing, beer-filled glasses raised to the sky.

It all looked quite fun, but Keira had a brief to stick to, so when she pulled her notebook out of her purse and began scribbling down some descriptions, they were all scathing—*gaudy lights, a poor-man's Vegas, nothing more than a nightclub spilled onto the streets.*

"What are you writing in there?" Shane asked as he parked.

Keira snapped her notebook shut guiltily. "Nothing."

Shane looked suspicious. But he didn't press it further. "We may as well get some food," he said. "This way."

Keira followed Shane through the throng of party-goers, some wearing crowns and sashes, all very drunk despite the fact it hadn't even fully gotten dark yet.

They stopped at a long picnic table that had been set up in the middle of the road beside a smoking barbecue. Plates of half eaten chicken and burgers lay strewn across the table.

"We're eating here?" Keira asked, raising an eyebrow at Shane.

"What's wrong? Too messy for you, Princess?"

Keira wasn't about to take the insult. In an attempt to prove herself, she sat down at the picnic bench, pushing a plate with crumbs and ketchup away from her. "I'll have a burger, thanks," she told Shane. "Well done."

He smirked and went off to order.

While he was gone, a group of young women came and sat at the picnic bench, sort of surrounding Keira. They were very loud. It was the perfect opportunity, Keira realized, to conduct some interviews. She turned to the girl next to her.

"Hi, sorry to interrupt," she began. "I'm a writer, working on a piece about the Lisdoonvarna Festival of Love. Do you mind if I ask you some questions?"

"Ask away," the woman said with a laugh and a hiccup. She was clearly tipsy. "I'm a seasoned pro here so a good person to ask!"

"Oh?" Keira said. "A seasoned pro? You mean you've been before?"

The woman leaned in and whispered loudly, "I come every year!"

"So you've never had a successful match?" Keira asked, pleased to have evidence to back up her position.

"Oh I've had a successful match, all right. I get a successful match with a new fella every year." She winked and nudged Keira. "Works quite nicely for me."

Keira started making some quick notes. That someone would use the festival like a dating app was very interesting to her.

"So you come every year just for a fling?" Keira clarified.

"That's a good way of putting it," the woman replied.

"Then you don't believe in The One?" Keira pressed. "In a perfect love match?"

"Of course not," the woman exclaimed. "It's the twenty-first century, there's no such thing anymore. The way I look at it, there's seven billion of us on this planet. What are the chances that you'll even find The One, supposing there is such a thing? Best to have the one, two, three, four... you get my drift." She started laughing again.

This was perfect, Keira thought. If even the attendees at the festival were critics the piece would practically write itself!

Just then, Shane came back with two burgers and a pitcher of beer.

"Not more beer," Keira groaned. "I can't handle this much alcohol."

Shane grinned. "You'll build up your tolerance soon enough. I bet by the end of the month you'll be drinking me under the table."

Just then, the woman Keira had been talking to leaned over.

"Aren't you going to introduce me to your friend?" she said, flashing seductive eyes Shane's way.

Keira couldn't quite comprehend the sudden surge of jealousy she felt. It was almost animalistic, instinctive. So powerful it was scary.

Shane leaned over her and offered his hand to the woman. "Shane Lawder," he said as he shook it, his eyes twinkling.

"I'm Tessa," she replied. "It's very nice to meet you."

"And you," Shane said with a wink.

For the first time, Keira got a flash of a side of Shane she hadn't yet been exposed to; the playboy side. She could see it in his eyes, in the way his pupils dilated. Shane got as much out of this festival as the rest of them. He probably had a fling once a year just like this woman did.

Keira leaned back as the two flirted over her, feeling a whole host of unsettling emotions, from generally grossed out to downright rage. She grabbed her phone, seeking a distraction.

On Instagram she found yet more pictures of Ruth's wedding. For the first time she felt somewhat lonely, and a little homesick. As she scrolled through the beautiful pictures, she stopped on one with a sudden jolt of surprise. There in the background was Zachary dancing with Ruth's friend Julia. And not just dancing, but *dancing*.

His hands were on the small of her back, which was bare thanks to the slinky, sexy dress she was wearing. Julia was leaning into him with a coquettish expression on her face. They looked like a couple, rather than just a couple of people dancing.

Keira felt instantly furious. Zach knew she'd see these photos. He'd purposefully done this to piss her off.

She fired off a message to Zachary, attaching the picture with the caption: *Jealous boyfriend grabs first available floozy.*

Then she grabbed the pitcher of beer and filled a glass. She took a deep swig. It was to become the first of many that night.

*

Keira wobbled her way down the street toward the B&B. She'd lost count of the number of beers she'd had, and the number of pitchers that had been purchased. It was a lot, and yet still not enough to numb her anger at Zach.

"Hey, wait up!" Shane called, following her along the street. "It's my job to make sure you get back in one piece."

He seemed remarkably sober for someone who had kept the drinks flowing all night.

"I'm fine," Keira mumbled. "It's not like I can get lost. There's only one road."

"Oh, it's like that, is it?" Shane laughed, taking her elbow to help steer her. "Are there not enough roads in Lisdoonvarna to satisfy Princess Keira?"

"I'm not in the mood to be mocked," Keira replied. The picture of Zach and Julia was still burned into her brain, still making her upset.

Shane backed off. "Okay," he said, his tone now more serious. "Well, here we are anyway."

They'd reached the door of the B&B. Keira fumbled with the latch.

"See you in the morning," Shane said as she walked inside.

She didn't reply, just wobbled her way through the heaving pub and up the rickety staircase to her room. Once inside, she flopped down onto the bed and sighed loudly. She kicked off her shoes and rubbed her sore ankles. It had been a long day. But it had also been inspiring. From her meeting with the matchmaker to the gray landscape of the Burren, from Shane and Tessa's amorous display at the festival to Zach's blatant attempts to make her jealous at the wedding, Keira wasn't low on snarky things to write about. Elliot was going to love this piece.

She just had to survive the rest of the festival.

CHAPTER SIX

Keira woke to a pounding headache and an overwhelming sense of embarrassment. She sat up and touched her head, wincing at the stream of daylight coming through the curtains. There was no way she'd get through this month if she continued to repeat this excessive drinking cycle.

Suddenly remembering the snarky text she'd sent to Zachary, Keira grabbed her phone, expecting to see an equally snappy reply. But there was none, which was even worse somehow. It was like Zach had cut her off entirely, like he'd broken it off with her without saying the actual words. Keira couldn't help but reassess her relationship, wondering if there was a relationship left at all.

Keira realized then that she'd somehow overslept and that Shane would be arriving any minute. A sense of panic swept through her as patches of memory resurfaced in her mind of her inebriated state last night, of her jealousy toward Tessa. Had she said something to Shane about it? Something that may have betrayed her attraction toward him? Her memories were too sporadic for her to rely on them.

Leaping out of bed, flustered, Keira grabbed her towel before realizing she didn't even have enough time to shower. She'd have to get through the entire day feeling grubby as well as hungover.

She dressed quickly, lancing pain shooting through her head with every hurried movement, then rushed downstairs.

"Morning," Orin said brightly from behind the bar as she emerged into the pub at the bottom of the staircase. "What can I get you for breakfast?"

"I'm so sorry, I'm in a rush," Keira said, yanking on her jacket. "I'll have to miss it."

The door opened then, and Shane came in. He was smiling contentedly and Keira wondered whether he and Tessa had enjoyed more than just a dance after he'd dropped her back at the B&B.

"Make sure you take this young lady out for breakfast," Orin told Shane. "She's missing the most important meal of the day."

"Honestly, I'm fine," Keira said. The thought of food was making her feel queasy. "I had a huge dinner last night."

Orin tutted and shook his head.

"We've got time," Shane said with a cheeky grin, grabbing a bar stool and sitting down.

It was as if he could tell that Keira's motivation for refusing breakfast was because of her hangover. He certainly liked putting her in awkward situations.

"I thought we had another day trip," Keira said through her teeth.

"We do, but it's just up the road," Shane replied. "It won't mess up our itinerary if we set off half an hour after schedule."

Keira had no arguments left, so she pulled up a bar stool and sat beside Shane.

"Excellent," Orin said, clapping. "What can I get you both? Eggs? Toast? Sausage? Bacon? Hash browns?"

"Toast, thanks," Keira said, selecting the plainest thing on offer that she might just be able to stomach.

Shane leaned into her. "He means all of the above," he explained. "It's called a fry-up. It's a great hangover cure."

Keira threw her arms up. She felt like there was no point arguing with these two. Between them they would make her obese by the end of the month. "Fine."

Orin disappeared into the kitchen to cook the fry-ups.

"Why aren't you hungover?" Keira asked Shane, leaning her elbow on the bar and propping her heavy head up on her hand. It came out like an accusation.

"Irish men don't get hangovers," Shane replied. When Keira gave him a look, he burst out laughing. "Isn't that what you're going to write in your piece? That we're all stereotypes with beer bellies?"

Keira just shook her head. Maybe in an hour or so, once the throbbing in her brain had subsided somewhat, she might be in the mood to deal with Shane and his constant teasing.

Delicious smells began to emanate from the kitchen and Keira's stomach rumbled in anticipation. Orin emerged with two enormous plates filled with food; fried sausages, fried mushrooms, fried tomatoes.

"That's quite a breakfast," Keira said looking at the plate in front of her. It was a long way from the iced green tea and spinach juice she usually grabbed on the way to the office.

"This is the secret to handling our booze," Shane said, laughing. "Start the day right and you'll be able to go all night."

Keira instantly tensed, wondering if Shane had been alluding to a night between the sheets with Tessa. She wanted to question him about it but knew she really had no right to. Plus, she didn't want to know what kind of emotion it might bring up in her.

They finished their breakfasts and went to get into the car. Remarkably, Keira felt significantly better. Her head wasn't pounding nearly as much as it had been on waking.

"So where are you taking me today?" Keira asked as they drove along the road through the now very familiar terrain, past debris left from last night's party.

"The Cliffs of Moher," Shane replied. "Ever heard of them?"

Keira shook her head. "Let me guess," she said, recalling the Burren from yesterday, "they're not actually cliffs."

"Oh, they're cliffs, all right," Shane said. "They filmed a bit of Harry Potter out here."

"Classy," Keira replied drily.

They drove out of Lisdoonvarna and along the narrow road, passing fields and hillsides as they went. Keira was too hungover for conversation, and so Shane put the radio on instead, where a female newsreader spoke Gaelic.

"Can you speak Gaelic?" Keira asked.

Shane gave her a look. "Of course I can. That's like asking a Spaniard if he can speak Spanish!"

Keira blushed and went back to her curled up position, gazing out at the rolling countryside.

The road was very bumpy, dipping at times in a way that made Keira's stomach flip. They were heading upward, spiraling and weaving up the tree-lined hillsides. Keira was glad she hadn't had to negotiate such a landscape on her drive from the Shannon airport; she might just have had a heart attack on the way. Shane, on the other hand, seemed very confident on the roads and he negotiated them expertly, which helped calms Keira's nerves, though she still felt like she was going to lose her breakfast any second.

Finally they reached the top of the hill and pulled into the parking lot. As Keira got out of the car, she saw an unusual building built into the side of the mountain with a grass-covered roof. It was a bit like a Hobbit house.

Wind ripped through Keira's hair and clothes as she walked beside Shane along the hilly terrain, using the flimsy railings around the cliff edge to guide them along the trail which overlooked the beaches below.

As they went, Keira thought it was breathtakingly beautiful, with a view that stretched on for miles and miles.

They stopped to take a breather, and Keira clung to the railing for support as she looked out at the raging ocean.

"That's the Atlantic," Shane explained from beside her. "Those are the Aran Islands," he added, pointing across the vast blue expanse. "And the other side there are the mountains." He crouched a little and came very close to her, pointing at a row of peaks she could just make out in the distance. "The Twelve Pin mountain range."

Keira felt her heart begin to race from the proximity to Shane. She took a step away, relieved to break the moment on one hand but instantly missing it and craving it again on the other.

"Want to go spelunking?" Shane asked.

"Is that when you swim in underwater cliffs?" Keira asked, raising an eyebrow. "I'll think I'll pass, thanks."

"You're not very adventurous, are you?" Shane accused her.

"Hey," Keira said with mock affront. "I'm an American abroad. Do you know how many of us never even get a passport?"

"Okay, I'll give you a point for having made it abroad. But I bet you've never climbed a cliff like this."

"Nor do I have any desire to," Keira said.

"Are you kidding me?" Shane exclaimed. "Climbing a beauty like this is incredible! It focuses everything down so narrowly. It's just you and the cliff. You and nature." His eyes were sparkling as he spoke.

"You've climbed this cliff?" Keira asked, not quite believing him.

Shane nodded. "And the Twelve Pins. Snowdon. Ben Nevis."

Keira was secretly impressed to discover this hobby of Shane's. But she wasn't about to let him know that. "Sounds a bit pseudo-macho to me. Man risking life and limb to conquer nature rather than just being at one with it."

Shane folded his arms. "And that's you, is it? At one with nature, Miss NYC?"

Keira looked away, ignoring him. They both fell silent, looking out to sea side by side.

Finally, Shane put his hands in his pockets and rocked back onto his heels.

"The sunsets here are the best you'll ever see," he said a little coyly. "If you didn't have to be at the festival every night I'd take you to see one."

Keira looked over at him, frowning. "That sounds suspiciously like a date."

Shane pulled a look of mock disgust. "You're barking up the wrong tree there, lassie, let me tell you."

Keira's cheeks tingled as she smiled to herself.

"So," Shane said. "What are you going to say in your piece about the cliffs?"

46

Keira looked back out over the beautiful scene. Just like before at the Burren, Keira felt a shift in herself, ever so slight but definitely perceptible. The air was so fresh compared to the polluted New York City air she'd known her entire life that it almost felt as if she were breathing in unadulterated oxygen, and it was making her giddy. Instead of craning her head to see the tops of skyscrapers, she was glancing out for miles at unbridled natural beauty, at nature unspoiled by man. Her ability to trash the place was wearing down.

"I don't know yet," Keira replied. "I'm having a bit of writer's block." It was the closest she could come to the truth without giving away the fact she was supposed to be mocking this place and the people within it. "Hopefully I'll get some good interviews tonight. The assignment is supposed to be first-person accounts, really. People's experiences of the festival. Whether they've found long-term love or not. Marriage. That sort of thing."

Shane smirked. "You don't think you'll find what you're looking for?"

Once again, Shane's question had some kind of underlying judgment contained within it. Keira had started to recognize the habit he had for doing that. It was almost as if he phrased statements and opinions as questions, forcing Keira to either refute or agree. She wondered whether it was an Irish trait, or specific to Shane.

She shrugged and leaned against her elbows on the railing. "I don't know yet. So far I see a lot of people having a good time. I don't know if anyone here is looking for love."

"What gave you that impression?"

"Well, it's all just drinking and eating, music and games. It's all a bit bachelorette party."

Shane laughed then. "You sound so disdainful."

"Because I am," Keira replied. "How do people think they're going to find The One when they're passing out drunk on Guinness every night? They'd have more luck coming out here into the real world. It's such a shame when they're surrounded by so much natural beauty."

She paused, and saw that Shane was watching her out of the corner of her eye. She didn't want to turn to him and fully take in his smug expression.

"I think our country might just be rubbing off on you," he said.

Keira ignored him. He was right but she certainly wasn't about to give him the satisfaction of knowing that.

"Anyway," Shane said after an uncomfortably long pause. "You'll have plenty of chances to speak to people tonight as I won't be at the festival getting in your way."

"You won't?" Keira said, looking at him for the first time in a while. She became aware suddenly of how much she wanted him there, how much his absence would be felt. The sensation shocked her in its ferocity.

Shane shook his head. "I can't. I have other things to do. And you know your way around now. You don't need me holding your hand."

Keira couldn't help but wonder about these other things he needed to do. Was it Tessa? Were they seeing each other again tonight? The thought ignited jealousy inside of her.

"I thought you were supposed to keep me safe," she replied. "Not leave me alone in the midst of amorous, drunk revelers. What have you got to do that's so important?"

Shane's face turned serious. He didn't answer her question. "I'd have thought you'd have gotten sick of me and want some time alone."

"Is that your way of telling me you've gotten sick of me?"

There was a pause, then Shane replied with, "Maybe a little."

Keira's mouth dropped open in shock. She couldn't tell if Shane was joking or not, but he certainly sounded serious.

"Have I said something to offend you?" she asked.

He shrugged nonchalantly. "Maybe."

Keira remembered the way Shane had become drawn and insular during their trip to the Burren. She'd put her foot in something then, offended him in some way, but he hadn't said how. Now she seemed to have done it again.

"Will you tell me what it is?" Keira said. "Because I seem to keep doing it and I don't know why."

Shane stretched up against his elbows on the fencing. He took a deep breath, then looked over at Keira. "If you must know, I have to pay my respects to someone," he said.

"Oh," Keira replied, deflating. Her voice softened. "Do you want to talk about it?"

Shane shook his head. "Not with you."

He turned then, heading along the trail, leaving Keira standing there shocked and confused. With no choice, Keira followed him, feeling wounded, unsure of what she'd said or done to provoke such a strong rejection from him. She walked the rest of the trail with her tail between her legs.

Back in her room later that day, Keira sat at her desk with her laptop open in front of her. She needed to get some work to Elliot and Nina but was struggling to find anything to say about the trip to the Cliffs of Moher. Not to mention her mind was still reeling from the offense she had somehow caused Shane.

Outside in the streets, the festival was gearing up. She could hear live music from a troubadour on the street corner. She began typing.

I hope to never hear the sound of an accordion again in my life. On my second evening, the sad sound of a lonely troubadour floats through the crack in my bedroom window. I wonder what he's done to alienate the rest of the musical community, why he's decided to go it alone when every other second person in Lisdoonvarna plays a violin or fiddle or banjo and takes every opportunity to join in and show off their skill. Perhaps the troubadour knows something the rest of us hapless romantics do not, or refuse to: we are alone and will remain that way.

She paused. It sounded catty. There was no creativity involved in berating this place and it was starting to make her feel bad. But it was the sort of tone Elliot seemed to like and so she carried on in the same vein before sending it off.

Elliot replied a few moments later.

This is great, Keira. Make sure you get some more interviews tonight. We need some more first-person accounts.

Keira sat back in her chair absorbing his words. It was the first-person accounts she was struggling with. It felt too mean to speak to people expressly for the purpose of bashing them later. But that was what she was here to do.

With a sigh she collected her purse, sliding her pen and notebook inside. She was going to miss having Shane by her side tonight, and her enthusiasm for the work at hand was starting to wane.

As she left her room and descended the staircase, Keira wondered what exactly this place was doing to her.

CHAPTER SEVEN

The festival that night was just as loud as the night before. More, in fact, since tonight was the beginning of the organized activities and competitions. The town never seemed to sleep when the Festival of Love was in session.

Keira chose a pub and went inside. It was still early but the place was already packed. She found a table in the corner and settled herself in, taking her notebook and pen out of her purse, then scoured the crowds looking for someone to approach. She wanted all different kinds of people, not just young women like Tessa who were just there for no-strings-attached encounters. What she really wanted was someone who was genuinely there to find love, someone who actually believed that they could be matched at this festival.

Just then, a man at the bar caught her eye. He was older than the average person she'd seen at the festival, with gray hair. She placed him closer to fifty. He was alone, sat on a stool watching the festivities as though he himself weren't really a part of them.

She stood and wended her way through the crowds until she'd reached the man. He looked a bit surprised to be approached by a young woman.

"Can I help you?" he asked in a thick Irish accent that Keira struggled to decipher over the noise.

She explained about who she was, why she was there, and asked whether he'd be willing to speak to her about his experiences of the festival.

"Sure, I've got nothing better to do," he replied. "I'm Patrick."

"Nice to meet you," Keira said. "I hope you don't take this the wrong way, but I couldn't help noticing that you're significantly older than the average person here. I was wondering what made you come here today."

Patrick laughed. "You mean I'm an old fart surrounded by beautiful women?"

Keira smiled and gave a shrug. "Your words, not mine."

"You can put that in your piece," Patrick added, tapping where she'd written the word fart in her notebook. He took a swig of his beer. "Okay, so you want my story. Here it goes. I'm older, yes, but it's not because I'm some horrible old pervert looking for a younger wife. There's plenty of men like me who find themselves without a partner at this stage of their life." He put his hand in his pocket and pulled out his wallet, then leafed through before pulling out a photograph. "This here is Susan. My wife of thirty years. Until she divorced me."

Keira wrote quickly, trying to decipher Patrick's accent.

"What happened?" she asked.

"Nothing, to be honest. The kids grew up and moved out. We both got older. I got comfortable, you know, let myself go, took her for granted. Then our business stalled and that meant the life I'd promised her never materialized. So she went off to find someone else who could provide it." He put the picture away.

"So you're here looking for some fun?" Keira asked. "Or some revenge?"

Patrick laughed. "I'm here looking for a wife!"

"You are?" Keira asked, wide-eyed. "You're not, like, over the whole marriage thing? Bitter? Jaded?"

"Of course not!" Patrick said. "I'm not bitter and I'm not over the hill yet. What I had might not have been enough for Susan but there'll be a lass out there who it will be enough for. Probably another divorcee." He laughed. "You get a lot of them coming here. That and widows. They're my best bet."

Keira was surprised. Her parents' own marriage had dissolved when she'd been very young, and her mother had lamented it for years. Watching her mom had meant that certain ideas were drilled into her head, and divorce was pretty much the worst thing she could imagine going through. It was a shock to meet someone who had not only gone through it but survived and come out the other end with their belief in love still intact.

"So you're planning on meeting with the matchmaker?" Keira asked.

Patrick nodded. "I already have. There was a lady in his book that he thought would be perfect for me. Eileen. She's forty-six, I believe, recently divorced also. Which means we've already got tons in common." He grinned.

"Are you going to meet with her?" Keira asked.

"That's why I'm here!" Patrick exclaimed. He smoothed his shirt down and his eyes lit up with excited anticipation. "I got in early so I could save us seats."

For the second time, Keira was shocked. She thought she'd singled out a lonely man in the crowd, watching on but unable to participate. Instead, she'd interrupted a divorced man waiting for a new date! Patrick hadn't been grateful for some company; Keira hadn't saved him from his loneliness. She'd merely been a way for him to pass the time while he waited for his date to begin.

The door opened then, and a woman in a beautiful emerald dress walked in. She was a similar age to Patrick, with gray hair covered up with blond streaks, a body that was bigger than the ideal. But she was glamorous, making the most of what she had, and looking very attractive for her age. She noticed Patrick and smiled.

"I should leave you to it," Keira said, backing off, feeling usurped, for the first time in her life, by an older woman.

Patrick's attention had already shifted to his date. He stood and kissed her on each cheek, then they both settled at the bar, the woman in the stool that Keira had just vacated.

Keira went back to her table and watched Patrick and his date as they chatted and laughed together. She noted the way she touched his hand as she spoke, and the sparkle in his eye as she laughed with abandon at one of his jokes. Once again, Keira felt another crack forming in her cynical wall. Maybe there was something to this. Maybe there were some people it worked for. Not someone like her, obviously, but for the older generation, ones who had already loved and lost and were ready to climb back on the horse again.

She stashed her notebook away realizing none of her interview with Patrick would make it into the final piece. The only way she'd be able to make it fit would be to turn him into a desperate caricature, something she was suddenly unwilling to do.

She would have to find someone else to interview, someone whose story aligned more closely with the cynical tone of the piece she was supposed to be writing. But everywhere she looked she just saw people enjoying themselves, people happy to be in new company, people who looked like they were falling in love. It was hardly the warts and all account that was supposed to be inspiring her. Instead, it left her with the most uncomfortable gooey, warm feeling inside.

Keira stood quickly before rushing out the pub and away from the claustrophobic atmosphere of romance.

*

Later that night, Keira received a welcome phone call from Nina. It was nice to get a taste of home, even if it was strictly on business matters.

"So Elliot loves what you've done so far," Nina told her. "And so do I. Your writing has dramatically improved for this piece. The tone you've taken is perfect. It's very evocative. I feel like I'm really there."

"Thanks," Keira said, smiling to herself.

"There is one thing, though," Nina said. "Joshua is out of the hospital and wants to dive straight back to work. But the doctors have signed him off for the month and he's not really supposed to come into the office. So Elliot thought it made more sense for him—Elliot—to take over the day-to-day *Viatorum* stuff and for Joshua to oversee the Ireland piece. Since he's on a ton of painkillers that mess up his sleep-wake cycle anyway, it means he can be more available for you. So basically Elliot isn't going to be overseeing the piece anymore."

Keira felt crestfallen. It was Elliot whom she'd wanted to impress, Elliot who held the key to her future career. Joshua would just take his usual approach to her work, of being derisive, dismissive, and critical.

Suddenly Keira felt as if the risk she'd taken in coming here might not actually pay off after all. How likely was it now for her to take that step up the career ladder? What if she ended up losing Zachary for nothing!

She ended the call with Nina and immediately phoned him. This silly game of silent treatment had gone on long enough. They needed to talk things through, properly, like grown-ups.

To Keira's surprise, the time zones must just have worked out because after several rings Zachary actually answered.

"I wondered how long it would take you to call," Zach said.

Keira frowned. "I've been in contact constantly. You're the one ignoring me."

Already she picked up on the combative tone. This was going badly and she'd barely even said anything yet!

Zach scoffed. "I didn't realize that photographs of sheep's butts and inbred soccer teams required responses."

"That's not all I've done," Keira replied cagily, feeling the need to defend herself.

"Oh, I forgot, there was also a drunk tirade. Thanks for reminding me." His tone was sharp, acidic, filled with venom. "You know, that's the sort of crap teenagers do, Keira. Sending drunk messages and stupid pictures. It's childish. This is the first time you've actually attempted to speak to me like a grown-up."

"If *speaking* was so important to you, why didn't you call me yourself?" Keira replied. She wasn't about to take the rap for their lack of communication over the last few days. At least she'd been trying. And Zach's condescending attitude was rubbing her the wrong way.

"Maybe because I was just having too much fun without you," Zach replied coolly.

A sudden jolt went through Keira. Something in his tone, the way he'd said it, had made her suspicious. "You mean with Julia?"

The other side of the line was silent.

"Zach?"

Keira felt a coldness spread all over her. His silence was speaking volumes.

"Zach, did you sleep with her?"

She heard him sigh. Then, finally, "Yeah."

Keira felt as if she'd been punched in the stomach. She couldn't catch her breath, so winded was she by his admission. She sat back against the bed, needing the support of the mattress beneath her to make it feel like the world wasn't dropping out from under her feet.

"I can't believe you'd do that to me," she stammered.

Zach sighed. "You'd gone and left me. I thought I made it clear that if you went to Ireland then I wasn't going to wait around for you."

"No, you didn't make it clear!" Keira yelled. "We argued, sure. You were pissed off. I get that. But I didn't think you were breaking up with me!"

"I wasn't," Zach replied. "You were breaking up with me. Remember? I said if you left I didn't think we could stay together. And then you left. As far as I was concerned, that was your way of ending it."

Keira fought for breath. Everything she was hearing was insane. Zach was trying to turn this all on her. He was trying to excuse his actions by making it seem as if she'd broken up with him. But as far as she was concerned, the words were never spoken between them to indicate that it was actually over.

"Even if you did think we'd broken up, it's not the classiest thing in the world to jump into bed with the first available woman," Keira hissed. Her voice came out hot, her tone accusatory.

"Do you know what, Keira?" Zach replied, sounding equally furious. "You're right. Julia was *available*. She was *there*. And that's a damn sight more than you ever were."

The call went dead.

Keira sat there holding the phone, finding it difficult to breathe. She hated crying but could feel now that there were tears streaming down her cheeks. She swallowed hard and found her throat completely constricted.

Had that really just happened? She'd never thought she'd hear such vitriol come from Zachary's mouth. For it be directed at her cut her to the core.

She realized then that Bryn hadn't been right about her and Zach at all. It wasn't a case of her and Zach being right at the wrong time, they'd just been wrong all along! Zach had just shown her a side of himself that she never knew existed, one that didn't support her achievements. He wasn't rooting for her success, he never had been. He just wanted a girlfriend who was *there,* putting him first, meeting his needs at the expense of her own.

It dawned on her then that Zach was a jerk. How had she never seen it before?

She crawled into bed and pulled the thin duvet up over her head. Outside in the street she could hear the noises of single people undertaking their continual search for companionship. For the first time in two years, Keira joined their ranks.

CHAPTER EIGHT

Keira was ready and waiting outside Orin's B&B bright and early the next morning. The last thing her broken heart needed was an Irish-style breakfast, so she'd made certain that there was no time for one, waking up with just enough time to shower and dress.

She stood on the street corner, her arms wrapped around her middle, feeling wounded by Zach's betrayal. She wasn't sure how she was going to get through today; all she wanted to do was curl up in bed and sleep. But when she saw Shane's car approaching, she felt a sudden sense of relief, as though her loneliness was melting away.

He pulled to a halt, mounting the curb beside the B&B, and Keira got in the passenger side.

"Morning," Shane said, stiffly.

Keira looked over at him, at his drawn expression, and suddenly remembered what he had told her yesterday about how he was going to pay his respects to someone, about how she wasn't the person he wanted to talk about it to. Her instinct was to ask him how he was, check in to see whether he needed anything, but the breakup had knocked her confidence, and Shane's rejection of her support yesterday stung more as a result. So instead of attempting to connect with him, she just stared absentmindedly out the window.

"Morning."

Shane pulled away from the curb and they began the drive. Keira wallowed in her misery, watching the dreary greens and grays that passed by through the window.

She wasn't sure how much time had passed before Shane finally spoke.

"You're quiet," he said.

"So are you," she replied, her gaze still fixed out the window.

"I suppose I am."

They fell into silence again. Keira hated it, the way their free and easy banter had been replaced by a huge, swelling nothingness.

"I spent the evening at a graveside," Shane replied by way of explanation. "What about you?"

"I'm just tired."

"There's something else."

She looked over at him at last. "It's none of your business," she said, echoing his sentiments from yesterday.

She didn't mean to be snappy, but talking about the breakup was the last thing she wanted to do right now. What she really wanted was a long chat with Bryn or her mom. Usually they'd be the first people she turned to when seeking comfort, but Bryn had been jogging when she called, and said she didn't have any time to chat, so she hadn't even had the chance to tell her about Zach. And with her mom there was a high likelihood that she'd use it as an *I told you so* moment. Keira hadn't been in the mood for that. Now speaking to anyone back in New York City was impossible because it was the middle of the night there. Keira hadn't felt so lonely since coming to Ireland as she did now. She could've done with offloading to Shane, but clearly neither of them was in the right place for that right now.

She turned her attention back to the view through the window and could feel Shane's eyes watching her. He didn't press it, though, and they fell back into their uneasy silence.

Unlike the other two trips, this one was much longer, and it gave Keira ample time to dwell in her misery. She decided that Shane was either respecting her lack of a desire to communicate or was too angry with her to want to try. Though his usual banter was conspicuously absent, he did keep looking over at her with a look of anguish.

Finally he spoke.

"Keira, are you annoyed with me for leaving you to attend the festival alone?" he asked.

She shot him a daggered look. "I'm not a kid, Shane. It's not like I'm giving you the silent treatment for rejecting me." She realized as she said it that that was actually half of the reason why she wasn't speaking to him. The realization took her by surprise. She folded her arms. "Why couldn't you, anyway?"

"I told you," Shane replied. His hands tightened on the steering wheel. "I had to pay my respects to someone. Someones, actually."

Keira couldn't help her curiosity. "Who?"

Shane took a deep inhalation, then let the breath go slowly. "I don't want to burden you with my stuff."

"I don't mind," Keira replied. Then, picking at the hem of her shirt, added, "It would take my mind off my own stuff."

Shane looked over at her. "Let's make a deal. I'll burden you, if you burden me."

Keira folded into herself. She wasn't ready to speak about the breakup. But on the other hand, she did want to know what was going on with Shane. Maybe it was a sacrifice worth making.

"Deal," she said finally.

Shane looked back out the windshield. The road ahead was narrow, but long and empty. It felt like they were the only two people in the world.

His hands still on the steering wheel, Shane briefly glanced over at Keira in the passenger seat. "None of this is going in your piece, okay?"

Keira held her hands in truce position. "Completely off the record," she confirmed, realizing once again as she said it just how much better suited Joshua would have been for this job. Nothing would be off the record for him. "So it must be to do with love, then," she said aloud as it dawned on her.

Shane nodded. "You're not going to like this. It goes against everything you stand for."

"Everything I stand for?" Keira said, frowning. "What do you mean by that?"

Shane cleared his throat and stared straight ahead through the windshield. "You made a comment about teenage sweethearts the other day."

"About how it always ends badly? You were offended by that?"

He nodded. "It was more the sound of complete contempt in your voice. The disdain. Like you could never believe it ever working out for two people."

"That's because I don't think it can," Keira replied. "In my experience, anyway. I mean the only people I know who married young divorced young as well. And if they stayed together it was only because their religion frowned upon their separating." She paused then. "Are you about to tell me you're with your teenage sweetheart?"

Keira was struck by how much the thought troubled her. She had never actually asked Shane whether he was in a relationship. She'd just assumed by his behavior that he wasn't. There was no ring on his finger, either, so he wasn't committed in that way, but what if there was some sweet girl waiting for him at home? One he left every year to come to the festival and party? The thought made her stomach roil.

"Sort of," Shane replied.

The sensation Keira felt then was akin to panic. Were all men cheaters? Did they all stray the second their girlfriends were out of eyeshot? How could someone *sort of* be with someone else, anyway?

Beside her, Shane seemed to deflate.

"She died," he said simply.

Keira felt a wave of guilt crash over her for ever doubting him, for letting her mind go immediately to her own place of hurt and paranoia.

"I'm so sorry," she gasped. "Recently?"

He shook his head. "No. It was a long time ago."

"What happened?"

"We met at school," Shane began. "Fell in love straightaway, although neither of us knew that's what it was when we were twelve." He smiled wistfully to himself. "We got older, started dating. Perfect is the only way I can describe it. I proposed before school was even over. She fell pregnant that night." Another smile, this time accompanied by a blush. "We were married at eighteen. Then one night, when she was eight months pregnant, the baby stopped kicking. We went to hospital. It had died." He gripped the steering wheel even tighter. "As she gave birth to our stillborn son, she died too. I lost them both in one night." He glanced at her sadly. "That's what I mean by sort of. 'Til death do us part. It just came a lot sooner than either of us expected. But she's still here." He touched his heart.

Keira felt cold all over. She'd never heard a story so tragic. "What was her name?" she asked gently. "If you don't mind telling me."

"Deirdre," Shane replied. "And I named the boy John, after her late father. I'm sure it's what she would have wanted."

Keira didn't know what to say anymore. She felt terrible, so filled with grief and empathy it felt like she might burst. What an awful experience to go through at such a young age. No wonder he'd been so annoyed at her high school sweetheart comment.

"That's whose graves you were visiting last night?" she asked, just as gently.

Shane nodded.

"Because it was the anniversary?" Keira asked. The thought that her words had been salt rubbed in the wound horrified her.

"No," he replied. "I only go when the urge takes me. It's usually several times a year, even now. I had that urge yesterday."

"Did something prompt it?"

He looked across at her then. "Guilt."

"Guilt?" Keira repeated. Then she realized what he must mean. His hook-up with Tessa. Being with another woman must have stirred up all kinds of emotions inside of him. At least, she thought that must be what he meant, though there was something else in his eyes that seemed unreadable.

"We're here," Shane said suddenly.

Keira startled. She'd almost completely forgotten they were in the car, driving to another location, so lost had she become in Shane's story.

They pulled up in the parking lot of a beautiful, stately home. It was a gorgeous old red brick building covered in crawling ivy. It hadn't been what she'd been expecting at all, although she realized now she hadn't even bothered to check her itinerary, or ask Shane where he was taking her today. She'd been so wrapped up in Zach she had completely forgotten.

"This is a bit fancy," she said.

"Muckross House," Shane told her. "It has gardens, lakes, and the grounds are now part of the Killarney National Park."

Keira looked out the windshield at the surrounding mountains. They looked blue in the thin daylight, like the backdrop of a watercolor painting.

"Want to go for a stroll?" Shane asked.

His tone was far more gentle than Keira had heard from him thus far. She didn't want to admit it, but it soothed her greatly. Maybe it wasn't Bryn's or her mom's comfort she sought to get her through the breakup. Maybe she wasn't looking for the care of a confidant but the touch of someone new and exciting.

She shook the thoughts away immediately. Hadn't she just told Zach about how unclassy it was to jump straight into bed with someone new as soon as a relationship ended? How could she now be having such similar desires? And hadn't Shane just told her about how much anguish and guilt he felt over being with other women? Not to mention he was her tour guide, paid for by her company! It was beyond inappropriate even to entertain the thought of hooking up with him. But there was a pull there, Keira had to admit.

They got out of the car. Keira saw something on the lawns and squinted.

"Is that a duck?" she asked, and a small giggle escaped her throat.

"Looks like it," Shane replied, smiling in response to the smile she'd finally managed to crack. "Must have wandered up here from the lake."

"Oh look, ducklings!" Keira cried, as a row of fluffy yellow chicks followed their mother, winding through the grass.

Keira cooed over the sight, then realized Shane was looking at her. This time his expression wasn't one she'd seen before from him. She saw something there in his eye, a twinkle. No, it was more like a burning. She wondered what William Barry would make of a look like that.

"I wanted to tell you how pretty you looked this morning," Shane said suddenly. "But you seemed so sad."

Keira was shocked to hear such words from him. He thought she was pretty?

"I was sad," she replied. "I still am."

Shane nodded. "I can tell. We made a deal, remember?"

Keira hesitated. It felt too dangerous to talk about romance and relationships, because she knew where her mind would go, what desires would be unleashed once she admitted to herself that she was back on the market. But the other side of her felt pulled toward that place, toward that slightly dangerous admission and the excitement that might result from it.

"Zach," she began. "My boyfriend. He's not my boyfriend anymore."

Shane looked genuinely sad for her. Keira could almost sense the way he wanted to comfort her, touch her and show her kindness. But he held back and she was grateful.

They began to walk again, ambling through the beautiful grounds of the old Victorian mansion.

"He cheated on me," Keira said after a long moment of silence. "I was supposed to go to his sister's wedding but I got put on this assignment. So he slept with one of the bridesmaids."

Shane gave her a sympathetic look. "I'm sorry. That sucks."

Keira pulled her arms tightly about her, as though trying to cradle the pain inside her ribcage.

"If it makes you feel any better," Shane said, "I'm really glad you came on the assignment."

Keira froze then. What was he saying? He'd acted so far like she was the most infuriating person he'd ever met. He'd even gone off with Tessa at the festival. Those weren't the actions of someone who cared!

"It's fun to have some company," he added quickly. Then with a shrug, he said, "I'm away from home as well. I tend to get a bit homesick over the festival, so it's nice to have a friendly face."

Keira realized then that she didn't know anything about Shane as a person. All she knew was his views on romance, and that his general outlook on life seemed to differ so much from hers. They'd jumped right into the debating, discussing the heavy stuff, and had never even had simple chitchat about their homes, their families, their friends, what they cared about.

"I don't know what to say to make it better," Shane said. "But I know it will get better."

She nodded and felt a little choked up. She'd felt a pull toward Shane before, even when he was being an infuriating jerk. Now she felt like a magnet was attracting her to him, making her move closer into his orbit.

"I would suggest a pint," he said with a sheepish grin. "But I have a feeling you won't like that."

She laughed and shook her head. "I'm already getting a beer belly," she laughed, patting her stomach.

"How about brunch then?" Shane said, and he pointed at a sign that told them there were tea rooms on the grounds.

"That sounds nice," Keira said. She hadn't had any breakfast and was quite hungry now.

They strolled along the path, following the sign to the tearooms, and went inside. It was a beautiful little building, probably the old caretaker's cottage now converted into a quaint cafe.

They sat at a small round table, their knees so close they were almost touching. Keira wondered suddenly if having brunch with Shane wasn't the most sensible idea. It was a bit like a date, she realized, only far more confusing.

They both ordered poached eggs on rye bread with coffees and juice. Keira tried to picture Joshua here, in this rustic tea room, with its delicate porcelain crockery. He would have stuck out like a sore thumb! Keira realized that she herself fit in much more here than she would ever have anticipated.

The food arrived and they began eating quietly. Keira noticed that Shane's expression was downcast, and it suddenly occurred to her that she'd been moaning on about her breakup when he had become a widower at the age of eighteen. He knew about love and loss far more than she did, had been through far worse than she now was. He must be thinking she was such a brat.

"I'm sorry for being so mopey," Keira blurted.

Shane shook his head. "No need. You're going through something rubbish."

Keira shifted in her seat. "But it must seem so juvenile to you. After everything you've been through."

"You mean because of Deirdre?" he said. There was a small smile on his lips. "You can say her name, you know. I wouldn't have told you about it if I didn't want to ever talk about it out loud."

Keira nodded, feeling suddenly privileged, like he'd let her in on one of his darkest secrets and she hadn't even realized the significance of it. "Yes. I mean after Deirdre."

"You might have noticed that after Deirdre I wasn't exactly a hermit," Shane said. "It's not like she's the only woman I've been with. I've had other girlfriends, some long term, some short. Caroline was my next big love."

"Oh God, what happened to her?" Keira asked, fearing the worst. Tuberculosis or the like.

"She cheated on me," Shane replied.

It wasn't the response Keira was expecting. That Shane had been through the same thing as her felt like another thing to pull them together. "Even though she knew about what you'd been through with Deirdre?"

Shane nodded. "Some people really can't see how their actions will affect others."

"That's remarkably diplomatic of you," Keira replied.

Shane just shrugged. "Well, I just think we're all a bit guilty of that."

Keira didn't think Shane's words were pointed, but it certainly applied to her situation. Zach had undermined their entire relationship by sleeping with Julia but she hadn't been exactly guilt free, either. She'd found it impossible to see his point of view about her work commitments, about the way she was always running off and prioritizing other things ahead of him. His actions had ended their relationship, but hers had shaken it in the first place.

"You said you missed your family earlier," Keira said. "How come you don't see them?"

"They just live quite far away from Lisdoonvarna," Shane replied. "Actually, they live kind of near here."

"You should take the day off," Keira suggested. "Go and see them!"

Shane shook his head. "I don't think I'd get hired again next year if anyone found out I'd shirked on my responsibilities. And I really need the money."

Keira felt bad for him. To miss people and be so close was the worst. She felt that in many ways with Bryn, with the way she was just on the other end of the phone and yet the time difference meant they couldn't talk.

"I have an idea," Keira said suddenly, her eyebrows rising. "Your job is to show me the real Irish life, right? Well, why don't you show me your hometown. Your family."

Shane almost spit his mouthful of coffee out. "I don't know if I'm quite ready to introduce you to my parents," he joked.

Keira rolled her eyes. "Shane, come on. I'm giving you a chance here. Using a loophole."

He didn't look convinced. "It's another hour drive from here. I don't know if we'd be able to get back in time for the festival this evening."

Keira thought about the woefully inadequate amount of interviews in her notebook, and the draft she had yet to send to Nina, of the pages of words she'd screwed up and thrown away because she no longer wanted to rip apart the people she'd interviewed. Missing a night of the festival would be pretty reckless. Unless…

"Are your parents still married?" she asked.

"Forty years going strong," Shane replied, smiling.

"Do you think they'd let me interview them?"

Shane looked surprised. "Well, they both love talking so I suppose so."

"There," Keira said triumphantly. "Your parents can be my interviewees for the evening. I have enough material to describe the festival and Ireland as a whole, it's the interviews I'm lacking on."

Shane seemed to suddenly brighten at the realization that she was serious, that this was really happening.

"Okay. Great! I'll call them now and let them know we're coming."

Keira smiled as he got up from the table and went outside to make the call. The only problem with this plan was that she was supposed to be tearing the myth of love and romance apart. But something had started changing in her. Her walls were beginning to come down. She was softening to Ireland, to the people, to the romance of it all. Especially now that Zach had broken up with her.

A thought hit her then. Elliot had wanted the piece to be firsthand, narrative driven, but what if she pursued a new direction, of the cynical New Yorker who suffers a breakup in the middle of a festival of love? What if she put her personal life, rather than just her views, front and center of the piece?

Just then Shane reappeared at the door. "You ready? My family are so excited to meet you."

"They are?" she asked, standing up and grabbing her purse.

She went to the door and followed Shane out.

"They're always happy when there's another woman in the house," he said over his shoulder as they walked back to the car.

"What do you mean another woman?" Keira asked, curious.

Shane grinned. "Oh, you'll find out soon enough."

CHAPTER NINE

The drive to Shane's hometown took them further and deeper into the heart of Ireland. Keira felt like she was being transported back in time, or through a wormhole to another universe where the grass was a more vibrant green, the air more oxygen rich.

"This is my town," Shane said, turning off the small road onto an even narrower one.

Keira looked about her, squinting in confusion. "But there's nothing here."

"Sure there is," Shane laughed. He pointed at a post box surrounded by hedges that had been untamed for so many years they seemed to be consuming it. "There's the post office."

Keira laughed. Shane pointed further ahead to a small wooden structure that looked like it might once have been a bus stop but hadn't been used for a decade.

"The local nightclub," he added. "Where teenagers meet to drink and dance and smooch. At least they would if there were currently more than one of them."

Keira couldn't help herself from dissolving into giggles. She found Shane great company and his wittiness was like a breath of fresh air for her, especially compared to Zach's seriousness. Keira checked herself; she really shouldn't be comparing her tour guide to her ex-boyfriend.

"What other sights are there in your bustling town?" she asked.

"Glad you asked," Shane quipped. "We have Doris the donkey in that field over there. She's older than me, believe it or not. A local celebrity. And here on your right is an actual off license."

"So the only shop in your town sells nothing but cigarettes and alcohol?"

"Correct," Shane said.

He slowed the car and Keira saw what he was indicating. They turned from the narrow road onto what Keira could only describe as a dirt path. The car bumped along the uneven surface.

"Um… just double-checking that you're not taking me to the middle of nowhere to murder me," Keira said, feeling a little uneasy for the first time.

Shane just laughed. "Of course not. Not with Doris there as a witnesses!"

Just then, the hedges growing on either side of the path thinned out. Keira saw that the fields on both sides of them were filled with animals and barns, troughs, tractors, and plows.

"Wait," Keira said, frowning. "You don't live on a farm, do you?"

"Yup," Shane replied, sounding excited by his proximity to his home.

Keira found his excitement infectious and became just as eager to see his home and meet his family.

"You weren't expecting a farm?" Shane asked.

"I suppose I should have," Keira laughed, surveying the fields filled with cows, sheep, and pigs. "You just don't give off particularly farmerish vibes."

"No?" he said, chuckling. "Well, you haven't seen me shear a sheep yet."

Keira raised an amused eyebrow. "And I can't wait to!"

They passed a row of barns and silos and then drew up in front of a large stone farmhouse. It looked to be several hundred years old, slightly wonky, the windows bowed with age. The stone was the same type she saw everywhere, dark gray, making the house appear to be at one with the surrounding landscape.

As Shane slowed the car to a halt, several young women burst out of the front door and began jumping up and down, waving, cheering, and clapping.

"Um…?" Keira began, feeling rather confused at the welcome committee. "You have a fan club?"

"Yup," Shane said, grinning. "They're my sisters."

Keira's eyes bulged with surprise. "*All* of them?"

"All six of them," Shane confirmed.

Now she understood what he'd met about there being another woman in the house.

He killed the car engine and flung his door open, quickly leaping out. The women pounced on him, covering him in kisses, jostling each other to hug him. Shane laughed gleefully, batting them away, wrestling with them in a way you'd expect to see between brothers. Keira couldn't imagine being so loved, or having so many people that happy to see her.

Finally, Shane found his way out of the clutches of his sisters. "Keira, these are my little sisters. I'll introduce them in age order but don't worry about remembering all their names, they tend to blur into one."

He smirked and one of his sisters smacked his chest.

"Watch your cheek, Shane," she teased.

Shane gestured to the woman who'd just smacked him. "Neala, my first sibling, my partner in crime."

Neala shook Keira's hand. "I'm younger than Shane but everyone thinks I'm the older sibling because, unlike my brother, I actually have a shred of maturity in my body."

Everyone laughed. Shane gestured to the rest of the women in turn. "Mary, Siobhan, Aisling, Elaine." Then he wrapped his arm around the shortest girl. "And the baby of the family, Hannah."

Keira thought that Hannah looked to be about sixteen. She had a youthful face that still showed signs of baby fat. Her hair was a beautiful golden blond, long and falling down her back in waves. All the sisters were pretty, but Hannah was strikingly beautiful.

"There are so many of you," Keira laughed.

"As there should be," Neala replied. "In a good Catholic family." She crossed her chest. The siblings dissolved into giggles.

It was obvious to Keira that this family loved each other dearly. And they seemed to look up to their big brother, both literally, since he was so tall, and figuratively. Their eyes practically gleamed with respect.

Just then, an older man and a woman came out of the door to the cottage—Shane's parents. Keira could see Shane in both of them, in the eyes of his father, in the coloring of his mother. He was like a perfect blend of them both.

Their eyes sparkled at the sight of their eldest child and only son. It made Keira's heart clench to see the love they had for him. Though she deeply adored her sister and mother, her own father was nothing more than a shadow from the past, someone she barely remembered. She wondered how different she would have become if she'd grown up in this sort of environment, surrounded by this much love. Would her views on romance be different? Would she be so hopelessly romantic like Shane seemed to think he was?

Shane's dad came up to her, his hand extended and a welcoming smile on his face.

"I'm Calum," he said. "You must be the young lady Shane's working for at the moment."

Keira blushed. "Oh, working for is a bit strong. He's my guide while I'm working on a piece about the Lisdoonvarna Festival."

"Keira's a journalist," Shane explained.

She shook her head, starting to feel embarrassed. "It's not as fancy as it sounds."

"Well, for a farmer from the depths of County Clare it sounds quite impressive," Calum said.

His gaggle of daughters laughed.

"Come on, you must come inside," Shane's mother said, ushering her with a welcoming arm. She spoke quickly, her accent thick and lilting. "Neala, put the kettle on will you, love? Keira will want some tea."

"Oh, you don't need to bother," Keira said.

Shane spoke to her out the corner of his mouth. "Let her make you a tea. You'll never hear the end of it otherwise."

Keira nodded then. "Okay, tea sounds lovely."

Shane's mom grabbed her arm and steered her into her house. "I'm Eve, by the way. Shane's told me all about you."

"He has?"

"Oh yes. He said he was very surprised that the magazine sent a woman. He'd been expecting a Joshua!"

"Ah, yes," Keira said. "Joshua broke his leg slipping on a macchiato."

Everyone erupted into loud laughter. The sound of it was joyously overwhelming to Keira. People didn't usually find her so amusing and it made her tingle with confidence. Keira already felt so comfortable here she was getting the feeling that she wouldn't want to leave when the time came.

Eve led Keira through the small corridors with low ceilings, past wooden staircases and doors so low that Shane had to bend down to get through them.

"Your house is gorgeous, Mrs. Lawder," Keira said.

"Why thank you, dear," Eve replied, patting her arm. "Calum grew up here, didn't you, love?"

Calum nodded in confirmation. "Eve lived in a house down the road. We met at church when we were three years old. I knew, even then, that I'd make her my wife one day."

"Dad," Shane complained. "Can you at least let Keira sit down before you launch into your life story?"

They entered the kitchen, which was like the sort of traditional old farmhouse kitchen Keira had seen on period dramas on TV, with wooden-topped work surfaces, cracked brick-red floor tiles, exposed ceiling beams (with an array of bronze pots hanging from hooks that had been bashed into them), and a messy arrangement of plants and herbs growing in teapots and broken mugs on the window ledge. It was so gorgeous Keira had to catch her breath.

Neala, the eldest sister, headed straight for the kettle to make the tea as she'd been instructed. The youngest sister, Hannah, took a cake out of a cupboard as if by magic, and started slicing it up.

"You'll have some cake, will you, Keira?" she asked.

"Not for me," Keira said politely.

Eve gripped her arm then. "You're not watching your weight, are you? A girl like you should be eating a slice of cake every day. Keep your hips round."

Keira dissolved into giggles.

"Ma!" Shane cried, looking embarrassed.

They all sat at the table. Neala brought over the teapot on a battered silver tray with ten mismatched porcelain cups sporting a faded picture of animals or a twisty flower design on them. They looked like they'd been collected over a period of decades.

"As our guest of honor, Keira, you may have the special swan mug," Neala said.

Keira didn't understand why everyone laughed then and assumed there was some kind of family in-joke she didn't understand. She wished quite strongly that she could be part of such a unit. She'd never realized how much she'd missed this until she was witnessing it. Compared to her home life it was so completely different. Compared to Zach's as well. It was a nice contract from the smug-faced Ruth and her oh-so-important wedding.

What was even more dramatic was the fact they all seemed to actually like her. They seemed genuinely impressed by her career, by her achievements, and awed by the fact she was from New York City. They fired questions at her, especially Hannah, who seemed the most enamored by Keira's lifestyle of all the sisters.

"I want to be a model," she explained.

Eve stroked her youngest daughter's long blond hair. "We'd prefer her to stay in Ireland but she's determined to move abroad one day."

Hannah suddenly brightened then. "Keira could chaperone me!"

Keira's eyes widened with surprise. She'd had just one cup of tea and one slice of cake and already she seemed to have been inducted into the inner sanctum of the family.

"Hannah, jeez," Shane said, rolling his eyes. "Can you not jump on the poor woman? Talk about putting her on the spot!"

Hannah pulled a face of mock offense. "Keira doesn't mind, do you?"

And Keira realized with surprise that Hannah was right. She didn't mind being jumped upon by this family of joy and happiness, and she certainly didn't mind feeling so respected and cared for. She couldn't remember the last time she'd been made to feel so *interesting,* or have her cheeks ache from smiling so much. The thought of having the bright, bubbly Hannah under her wing in New

York City was an idea she was surprised to find herself loving. She wanted to be part of this family. To never leave.

She had fallen in love with this place, this feeling. Maybe there really was such a thing as love at first sight.

Just then, Eve reached across the table and took Shane's hands in hers.

"I have a very serious question to ask you," she said.

Shane looked suddenly pale and afraid, like he was expecting something awful and bracing himself.

Eve's face cracked into a huge grin. "What have you done to your hair?"

Everyone burst out laughing.

"I'm glad you said it and not me!" Mary laughed. "You look like a scarecrow, brother."

"I was thinking the same," Neala exclaimed. "Come on, let's get you trimmed and shaven."

She grabbed him and jostled him to standing. Shane turned a bright shade of red.

Eve tutted and shook her head at Keira. "He's terrible. So used to having a woman there to keep him in line. If it's not a mother it's a sister, if not a sister then it needs to be a wife." She laughed.

Keira laughed too, and waited with anticipation for the big reveal.

*

While Shane was off having his makeover, Keira took the opportunity to speak to Eve and Calum about their love story. She got out her notebook and pen.

"So you met when you were three, is that right?" Keira began.

Calum nodded. "Love at first sight. For me anyway."

"What about you, Eve?" Keira asked.

"Goodness, no. I thought all boys had germs," Eve said with a chuckle. "And continued to think as much until I was approximately fifteen years old."

"What happened when you were fifteen?" Keira asked.

"I was kissed by a boy," Eve said. She reached out and touched Calum's hand. "This boy!"

Keira scribbled down their story, which she found quite delightful. "So it's only ever been the two of you? You've only ever had eyes for each other?"

They both nodded. Keira once found these stories suspicious, but she was starting to accept that they were real, that there were

70

some couples who didn't embellish their love stories or pretend their marriages were happier than everyone else's.

Keira took a sip of her freshly brewed cup of tea. "So, what's your secret? How have you made it last for so long?"

It was Calum who spoke. "It helps that we have a lot of similarities. Our faith, for example. We both have lots of siblings so we always knew we wanted to have as many kids as God chose to bless us with."

Eve interjected. "And we were both raised on a diet of meat and potatoes so there's never any arguments about what to have for dinner!"

Keira laughed. She found Eve and Calum refreshing. They were so grounded, so filled with humor and light.

"But didn't either of you want to see more of the world? Maybe try living in a city for a while?"

Calum shook his head. "It just wasn't done when we were growing up so it never crossed our minds. Holidays abroad were things rich people had. For us it was an annual trip to a campsite in Kerry! If we were lucky."

Keira wrote her notes down and considered their words. Was it easier in the past to find true love, without all the cultural influence and tempting opportunities people like she now had? Was that the compromise her generation had to make for the way technological advances had shrunk the world? Eve and Calum had never had to argue about how many kids they wanted, let alone whether they wanted any at all! They never had to deliberate about uprooting the family for a job opportunity far from home. In many ways their paths had been set out for them. Provided they followed those paths true love was more or less an inevitability.

Keira was on her third cup of tea when she heard the sound of footsteps thundering down the staircase that indicated Shane's pampering session was complete. She put her notebook away and turned in her chair, looking over her shoulder at the door to the kitchen. Eve looked up from her cup of tea.

"Oh my!" she exclaimed as Shane emerged from the shadowy hallway into the room.

Keira's eyes widened and she stifled a gasp. Without his chin hidden by straggly hair his strong, pronounced jawline was on display. After his eyes it was probably his most attractive feature and Keira wondered why he'd hidden it under a beard. His hair had been trimmed short and close to his scalp. Either his sisters were very talented at cutting hair or Shane had the sort of forgiving face that could carry any style whatsoever.

Keira felt a tingle deep inside of her. It was so alarming to her she had to avert her eyes from Shane.

"Doesn't he look gorgeous?" Eve exclaimed, nudging Keira across the table. "Take a look at him!"

Keira flicked her gaze up shyly and smiled. "It's nice."

"What do you mean nice?" Eve cried with unflagging enthusiasm. "He looks like a film star!" She jumped up from the table and rushed to Shane, then kissed him on both his cheeks.

Shane's sisters crowded behind him, laughing and looking very pleased with themselves.

"What do you think, Keira?" Neala asked. "He'll be getting hitched in no time with his new do."

Shane turned a deeper shade of crimson. Keira felt uncomfortable suddenly, realizing that Neala was right. Clean-shaven Shane was even more of a catch then the scruffy Shane had been. He would have women lining up to date him on his return to Lisdoonvarna.

Shane took a big step forward then and Keira realized one of his sisters had shoved him closer to her.

"Shane, when are you taking Keira on the tour of the farm?" she said, her tone one of urging.

Shane scratched behind his neck nervously. "Well, I don't know if Keira wants a tour of the farm," he said, suddenly shy.

"Of course she does," the same sister said. "Don't you, Keira?"

"Sure," Keira said. "That sounds nice."

"Fine," Shane said a little stiffly. "Why don't we go now?"

He gestured for Keira to take the lead down the corridor, and brought up the rear behind her. Keira could hear the loud whispers of his sisters as they went.

They reached the front door and Shane opened it up for Keira. Once he was also out the house he shut it behind him and took a deep breath.

"I'm sorry they're so crazy," he said.

"Don't be," Keira replied. "I loved it. I've never felt so welcome."

Shane smiled shyly. "Hospitality is certainly one of their fortes. How many cups of tea were you force fed while my sisters cut my hair?"

"Only three," Keira said.

Shane laughed. "Thanks for swinging it so we could come here," he said. "I didn't realize how much I missed home."

"No problem," Keira replied, confident that the benefits had definitely been greater for her.

They walked along the path, passing fields of corn and wheat, sugar beets and lettuce.

"Your farm is amazing," Keira said. "I can't believe you got to grow up in a place like this."

"Bit different from NYC, huh?" Shane teased.

It was the first time he'd mocked her all day, and it occurred to Keira that he'd been keeping the teasing on the down low. She wondered if that was out of respect for her bruised heart. She couldn't be sure but she certainly had appreciated having a bit of a break from the constant barrage of put-downs!

"Here, follow me," Shane said, suddenly grabbing her hand.

Keira felt no instinct to let go. In fact, her hand in his felt comfortable, like it always was supposed to be there. His hands were big and rough and warm, and her own smooth, delicate ones seemed to fit perfectly inside them.

He pulled her gently along, suddenly alive with energy. She followed him, skipping to keep up, until they were both full on running through the fields. The wind whipped through Keira's hair and her cheeks stung from the cold. She'd never felt so awake and alive.

Shane led her to a small stream beneath a weeping willow. The leaves surrounded them, creating a tent like environment. He sat down, pulling her down with him.

"This is a great spot to watch the sunrise," Shane explained.

Keira realized then how dark it had become. The whole day had passed her by and she hadn't even noticed. She'd been so filled with excitement and fun that the hours had disappeared from her.

She checked her cell phone and saw she'd missed several calls from Bryn. Her sister had also texted her a stream of photos of attractive men to cheer her up. She laughed aloud, somewhat shocked to discover she hadn't needed her sister to cheer her up after all, that the company of a good Irish family and their copious amounts of tea had the power to lift her from her gloom.

She looked through the leaves of the willow at the sky as it turned pink and purple. It really was beautiful.

"Have my parents given you any good material for your article?" Shane asked, breaking through her reverie.

Before Keira had a chance to reply, she felt her phone vibrate in her pocket. She looked at it and saw that an email had arrived from Joshua. Her heart instantly sank.

She quickly read the message.

Nina told me you wanted to change course on the article, make it about you and your boyfriend's breakup. I think it's a stupid idea.

She's shown me what you've written so far and though it's a pitiful amount it's better than your suggestion of changing course. No one wants to read about your drama. Is that what you've been doing over there all this time, crying about your breakup? I want a new draft in my inbox by the morning.

Keira wanted to write back and tell him, hotly, that she'd been given an impossible assignment, but she swallowed her frustration and stowed her phone back in her pocket.

The email made Keira's happiness shatter. How could she rip this place apart now? There was no way she could turn Eve and Calum's love story into a sappy romance. No way she could tear apart the festival that brought so many lonely and desperate people together, giving them second chances at love that had, for a variety of reasons, been stolen from them.

But she had no choice. She had to write the scathing piece she promised Elliot and Joshua. The one Nina was pushing her in the direction of. And the thought made her hate herself.

"I don't know if their story will make it into my final draft," she mumbled.

"Why not?" Shane demanded. "It's great. Hollywood film stuff."

Keira shifted uncomfortably, wanting desperately on one hand to reveal to Shane the real tone her piece would take but knowing to do so would shatter his trust in her.

"Well, next time I'm submitting a script to Hollywood I'll consider it," she said, trying her best to cover her discomfort with a joke.

Shane laughed and dropped the subject. He turned his face from her, looking out the leaves of the willow tree at the sunset. She studied his face, taking in the contours his trimmed beard had revealed, feeling suddenly like she was double-crossing him, like a snake who couldn't be trusted.

CHAPTER TEN

"Are you sure you need to travel back tonight?" Eve said, holding onto Shane's hands. "It's ever so dark now."

Shane nodded. "We'll be fine, Ma. Don't worry."

He pulled open the driver's door but didn't get a chance to get inside because his sisters tackled him from behind.

"Stay!" they cried.

"We want to have a sleepover with Keira," Hannah whined.

Keira desperately wanted to stay the night—for the rest of her life, if she was being honest with herself—but her anxiety over her piece was starting to rear its head again, no thanks to Joshua's curt email. Only now the pressure was even worse because she was wrestling with the addition of feelings of self-loathing.

"I'm sorry," Shane told his youngest sister. "But I'll bring Keira back another day, okay? She's here for the whole month, after all."

"Are you, Keira?" Hannah squealed, looking more excited than ever. "Will you come back next weekend?"

"I don't know about that," Keira said. "If my work is going well then I can. I'm a bit behind at the moment." Saying it aloud made her feel it more keenly, and her stomach sunk.

"Not everyone spends their days skipping through buttercup fields, sis," Shane said drily to Hannah. "Some people have to work."

His little sister pouted. Shane pulled her into a bear hug. "I'll see if I can convince her to another trip later."

Keira couldn't help but feel rather mournful at the thought of a missed trip to see the family. She wished she'd met them all under completely different circumstances, perhaps as a traveler or wandering nomad type, then she could stay guilt free on their lovely farm for as long as she wished. As it stood, she felt an overwhelming sense of guilt about the piece she was supposed to be writing. How could she insult this wonderful place that created such delightful humans as Shane and his family? And how disappointed would they be when they read her words in print, bashing them for being simple? She felt sick with anxiety.

Finally, they got back into the car and Shane waved his final goodbye to his family. He reversed the car out of the drive and turned them around onto the small dirt path. There were no streetlights and Keira found the darkness somewhat suffocating.

Even when Shane turned out onto the main road, which was at least made of asphalt, she still felt the blackness crowding in on her.

"You okay?" Shane asked.

Keira nodded.

"Are you mad that I kept you away from your writing for so long?" he said. "We won't get back until about midnight at the earliest."

"It's not that," Keira said.

Shane fell silent, turning his attention back out the windshield.

"Is it Zach?" he asked after a long moment.

The pit that was already in Keira's stomach grew. She hadn't given Zach so much as a second thought all afternoon. She'd allowed herself to get completely sucked into the magic of Shane's family home. Now it felt like reality was back to bite.

"It's work," she said dismissively.

"Writer's block?"

"Something like that."

Shane gave up trying to get Keira to talk. She slumped in her seat, resting her chin on her fist and watching the hedges zoom by out the window. She felt like she'd blown everything, her writing and things with Shane. What a mess it all was.

"I'm sure you'll find someone to speak to tonight," Shane said hopefully. "Maybe the horse race will give you the spark of inspiration you need."

"Horse race?" Keira asked.

Shane looked at her and grinned, his cheeky self seemingly returning. "You haven't heard about this? It's bonkers. And great fun. It's curated by the matchmaker. He puts couples together and then they race in a horse and cart."

"Like gladiators?"

"Sure. But very slow. It's really fun. You'll love it."

Keira thought she probably would, just like she seemed to like everything else in this country. And that was just the problem.

*

When they made it back to the festival it was indeed very late in the evening. They parked and headed into the crowds.

A band played country music as Shane led Keira over to one of the stalls. There were two huge shamrock piñatas sat upon it, one pink and one blue.

"A confusing mix of cultures," Keira said. "What is this? Some kind of baby shower contest?"

76

"You pay a euro to put your name in the piñata and at the end of the festival one man and one woman win a prize," Shane explained.

"A romantic trip for two," the lady manning the stall said.

Keira rolled her eyes. "I'm good, thanks."

Shane pulled some money out of his pocket and paid for two slips, writing his name on one and Keira's on the other.

"Good luck!" the lady behind the stall said as he posted them into the piñatas.

Keira tutted and shook her head. "What a waste of money," she said to Shane.

He just shrugged. "You've got to be in it to win it."

She looked at him with a frown. "Who wants to go on vacation with a stranger?" she scoffed.

She could hear the tone of her voice. The pressure was getting to her and it was starting to bubble over, to spill out as irritation. Poor Shane was just in the way of her bad mood.

They followed the crowd of people to the side of the street where a barricade had been put up. Standing in the street the other side stood several horses with carts attached behind them, the type that people could stand up in. There was bunting strung across the street.

"Looks like it's starting soon," Shane said. "Fancy a go?"

"Us?" Keira exclaimed. "No way. I have to do some more interviews. Like yesterday. My jerk of a boss is on my back."

"I could help," Shane said. "Look for some people?"

Keira shook her head. Shane had no idea what kind of people she needed for the interview. He'd probably pick the cutest most loved up couple ever, not realizing that what she needed were two poorly matched people in a train wreck of a relationship.

Instead, she rummaged in her purse and pulled out some euros. "Why don't you go?"

"Alone?" Shane said, surprised.

"Ask one of the singletons to ride with you," Keira insisted. "It won't be hard to get a date with your swanky new hair." Then under her breath she added, "Find yourself another Tessa."

Shane looked horrified. "I'm not doing that," he stammered.

Keira wondered what was provoking such a reaction in him. She dared not let herself believe it could have anything to do with her. But even so, she couldn't help but feel a flutter in her stomach at the fact that Shane was refusing. Things had definitely changed since that first night with Tessa.

"Well, place a bet for me then," Keira said, nudging the money his way.

"On who?" Shane asked, bemused, as he took the money from her.

"On the horse with the silliest name," she said. "I'll listen for it on the speaker."

Before Shane had a chance to argue, Keira rushed off into the crowd, detaching herself from him like a Band-aid on sensitive skin. Leaving him left a sense of longing inside of her, one she loathed and loved in equal measures.

Desperate to find someone who fit the bill for her article, Keira wandered into a nearby pub. But inside she just found more of the same, more happiness, more romance, more joy. She knew not to trust forlorn men at the bar because of her experience with Patrick. So far, Tessa was the only person whose interview had any worth to fitting her narrative.

She went outside, looking for another hen party group, some drunk young women who were just here to play the field. But it seemed as though the matchmaker had done his job too well. Everywhere she looked she saw happy couples, men and women looking loved up in each other's company.

Over the loudspeakers, the horse race was announced as about to start. Everyone's attention seemed to be focused on that. Keira realized that the only place she wanted to be right now was beside Shane, watching along like all the others. No one would know they were working together; they'd look just like any of the other couples here. The thought made her stomach flutter.

She weaved back through the crowds. When she saw the back of his head, she made a beeline, then nuzzled her way in beside him.

"That was quick," he said, looking down to see who had nudged him out of the way.

Keira shook her head. "I can't find anyone for my article. I don't know what to do."

"Can't find anyone?" Shane mocked. "You're surrounded by loved up couples."

Keira sighed. There was no way she could tell him her article was supposed to trash this place. She hated to think how little he would think of her if he found that out. And besides, she was going to have to change tactics. There was no way she could complete the article in the way Joshua and Elliot wanted her to.

"Well then, maybe I just wanted to see the race more than I wanted to work," Keira said. "Who did you place our bet on?"

"I went for these two," Shane said, pointing to a carriage that contained an old man and old woman who must have both been in their eighties. "Their anniversary falls on the festival so they come and celebrate whenever they can. Isn't that sweet?"

Keira laughed aloud. It no longer surprised her. She was surrounded by fairytale love stories.

The race began and the horses started trotting along the road. It wasn't exactly the Grand National but it was definitely entertaining. Keira jumped up and down, cheering them on, clapping along with Shane. She couldn't wipe the grin from her face, in spite of the anguish she felt over the article, over her career.

Her phone buzzed, tearing her out of her reverie and reminding her, just as she was about to get comfortable, that there was work to be done. Luckily it wasn't Joshua this time, but a message from Nina.

Sorry if Joshua bites your head off about the article, I might have let slip that you were struggling to fit the brief.

Keira quickly typed back that it was fine, she expected no less from Joshua, and that she'd find a way to make it work to his taste.

As soon as she'd fired off her email, Keira returned to the temporary state of calm she'd found with Shane. What was it about this place that changed her so drastically? At no other point in her life would the sight of the slowest horse race in the world make her laugh with abandon, or the constant supply of tea and cake from a warm Catholic family make her feel such grand affection. Something about Ireland made her feel genuine, less jaded and stuck up, more alive and enthralled by life than she had in years.

The elderly couple Shane had placed the bet on didn't win. Instead, the race was won by an attractive middle-aged couple. William Barry was there to hand them their trophies and crowns, which were both inflatable.

Keira wondered whether this might be a good angle for her piece, and decided to take the opportunity to speak to them. She nudged her way to the front.

"Can I get an interview with you guys?" she asked.

The woman looked at her a little bemused. "What for?"

She had a European accent, Keira thought. Polish, perhaps.

"I'm a travel writer for a magazine in America. I'm writing a piece on love and romance."

"Watch out for this one," William quipped. "She's a cynic."

The couple exchanged a glance, then shrugged their agreement. Keira led them to a nearby picnic table.

"So the obvious question is where do you come from?" Keira asked. "I can tell by the accent you're not a local."

The woman laughed. "I'm from Krakow."

"And you came to Ireland specifically for the festival?"

The woman nodded seriously. "To find a husband."

Straight to the chase then, Keira thought. She wrote her notes quickly. "So you were both matched this evening, specifically for the horse race?"

The woman nodded. "I've been at the festival since the beginning. William was waiting to find me the right match. I had to be patient. Then today it happened."

The man beside her grinned. Keira noticed they were holding hands under the table.

"Do you think William made the right call?" Keira asked. "You're happy with the outcome?"

"Very." The woman nodded, looking thrilled.

The man seemed just as pleased. "I wouldn't have come if I didn't trust him to do a good job of it."

"So you believe in all of this? In the romance? The love?"

The woman nodded, and flashed an amorous look toward her new beau. Walking behind them, Keira caught sight of the old couple, the one that Shane had placed their bet on. They seemed lost in each other, almost oblivious to the hubbub around them, as they strolled along the street hand in hand. She wondered how many of the couples who'd been matched this year would become that elderly pair one day. Before she came here she would have put the figure at less than one percent. But now she wasn't so sure. Maybe even the couple sitting in front of her would become them some day! Keira wasn't starting to think that everything seemed possible.

"When do you both leave?" Keira asked.

"Tonight," the man said. "Now we've been matched there's no reason to hang around."

"And what happens next? Will you keep in touch?"

"I'm taking her home with me," the man replied. "Back to Dublin."

Keira laughed, thinking he was joking. But when she looked at the woman she realized by her expression that he was deadly serious. Had she met this couple at the beginning of her stay she would have scoffed at them, thought them irrational, illogical. But now after everyone she'd met and everything she'd seen, she found herself rooting for them, wanting everything to work out for them.

She snapped her notebook shut. This was useless. She was never going to get the material she needed for her article.

"Thanks, guys," she said to the couple. "I wish you both the best of luck."

But they seemed to have already forgotten about her, their eyes only for each other.

Keira went back to the B&B. The detour to Shane's house had been a bad idea. It had taken lots of time out of the time she devoted to the festival, and she had hardly left herself any time to write.

Her phone began ringing and she saw that Bryn was calling.

"Hey, lil sis," she said when Keira answered. "I'm so, so sorry about Zach."

It already felt like a lifetime ago that she'd been dumped. Had it really just been one day?

"I think I might be over it," Keira said.

Bryn started cackling. "Nice. Do you need me to go over to the apartment and collect some stuff for you?"

It hadn't yet occurred to Keira that she wasn't just single, but homeless. She'd have to find somewhere new to live when she got back to New York City.

"That would be great if you could," Keira said.

"You really don't sound as upset as I was expecting," Bryn said suspiciously. "Is something going on?"

Keira flopped onto the bed and sighed. There was no point keeping it from Bryn. "It's Shane. I think I'm falling for him."

"Oh. Wow. Really?"

"Yeah."

"You just mean that you want to sleep with him, right?"

"No, I mean I want to be with him. His partner. We just spent the day with his family and it was so much fun. I fell in love with the place, with them. He has six sisters. Six! And they're all amazing. But his youngest sister is sixteen. Her name is Hannah. I think we really connected, you know. There was a real bond there."

Bryn was silent. Then, "Keira, you've known him less than a week. And he's already had a one-night stand in that time. You can't trust this guy."

"What?" Keira snapped. "I thought you of all people would be encouraging me."

"To have a rebound fling, sure," Bryn said. "Not to go from being tied down to some jerk to being tied down to another. You don't even live in the same country. It would never work."

Keira sighed, irritated.

"I don't mean to be the harbinger of bad news all the time," Bryn added. "But it's my duty as your sister to call you out on this stuff. You like Shane because he's a sexy, Irish, mountain-climbing, fiddle-playing bloke. He's fling material. End of. He's probably good for a few rolls around in the sack and nothing more. And I'm sorry if you think he wants anything different from you, Keira, because he doesn't. He knows how to play the system. You already said so yourself."

It hit Keira then that Bryn was right. She'd been getting carried away with herself. She knew guys like Shane back in America. They were the kinds of guys Bryn went on dates with. She'd been burned so many times thinking a guy was really into her when he was actually really into the idea of sleeping with her. Shane was a player, she'd already seen evidence of it.

"Keira?" Bryn asked.

"Sorry. I'm just... I guess you're right. Maybe he only seems great because Zach's been such a jerk."

"See?" Bryn said. "Flirt away with him, sis. Have your fun. Just don't think it's more than it is."

With her sister's sage advice streaming through her head, Keira ended the call and got to work on some writing. She tried to emulate the snarky tone she'd captured so well on her first night here, but even as she read over the first draft she couldn't reconcile herself with the person she'd been back then. She closed her eyes and thought of Zach, of how angry she was at him, and tried to channel those emotions into her writing, but to no avail.

An email came through from Joshua, with just one simple word: *Update?*

The pressure certainly wasn't helping. She shuffled over to the window and tried to eavesdrop on some of the conversations taking place on the streets beneath her, tried to conjure up her irritation during those first few sleep-deprived evenings when the noise had kept her awake. But it was useless. Even the disgusting wallpaper now just seemed quaint to her. All the chatter was more like soothing white noise rather than grating.

She closed her eyes and immediately saw Shane's face floating into her vision. Then she heard a noise coming from the window beside her. Her eyes snapped open and she looked left just in time to see a pebble hit the window. Down in the street, bathed in moonlight, stood Shane.

Shocked, Keira pulled open the window.

"You ran off without saying goodbye," he called up to her.

"I'm sorry," she called back down, acutely aware of how much her heart was racing. How could she tell him she'd needed space? That she was finding it hard to tear herself away from him but desperately needed to get some work done?

"Well, are you saying goodnight now or are you coming down for the next horse race?" Shane shouted.

With his new trimmed beard and styled hair, none of his gorgeous features were obscured. Bryn's warning repeated in Keira's mind, not to get to close, to have fun but not to fall for this guy.

Fun. She deserved that, right?

Keira leapt out of her seat. "I'm coming," she called down.

She shut the window hurriedly, excited to be reunited with Shane. Then she snapped her laptop closed, shutting away Joshua's demanding email.

CHAPTER ELEVEN

Keira spent the rest of the evening in a happy daze. There was something about being in Shane's company that made her feel carefree and relaxed. It was exciting to have someone to flirt with, to feel those tingles of desire, even if it felt like her work was suffering as a result.

The next day he took her to the annual Irish Barbecue Championships, an event that turned out to be very conducive to writing, since it was filled with competitive men trying to impress single women with little more than their ability to shovel copious amounts of meat into their mouths.

After several hours at the Barbecue Championships, it became impossible to tell apart the pink-faced, round-bellied, mucky-mouthed males from the pigs they were munching on. If a drunk female walks home with her arm slung around a hog roast declaring her undying love, I don't think I'll even be surprised.

When Nina received that update email—along with some accompanying photographs that Keira had taken of a group of chubby, drunk guys holding up barbecued chickens thighs, looking somewhere between cheery and menacing—she was thrilled.

More of this, please! Except I want to see what would happen if you dated one of them. Time to get your hands dirty, Keira!

The thought of dating one of those oafish lads repulsed Keira. So she found the next best thing: Lisdoonvarna's Speed Dating Event! She'd never done anything like speed dating. The thought of it made her cringe. And this was speed dating on a massive scale. Fifty participants! It took her two large sauvignon blancs to build up the courage to do more than just observe and take notes. But once she took the plunge, she discovered it a far quicker route to procuring usable information. Nina was right, getting her hands dirty was a good approach.

Keira had three minutes to speak to each man before a bell was rung to signal that they needed to move on. By the end she'd got her opening gambit down to a simple, "I'm a reporter. This is a tape recorder. Okay?"

It ended up being several grueling hours of listening to men drone on about their various careers, their hopes, their dreams.

Each face melds into the next. I'm certain I've already spoken to Craig, the plumber from Dublin. But no, that is Craig, sitting across the hall from me, presumably repeating his spiel about being good with his hands to a woman who looks as equally unimpressed with him as I was. Which means this is a different man I'm talking to. "I'm sorry, I've forgotten your name," I admit. This is Carl. He's also a plumber from Dublin. And he is to be just one of dozens of plumbers I meet that evening...

Nina responded just as positively to that piece. Bryn, on the other hand, replied with, *You should have gone for it, sis. I bet that Craig guy really* is *good with his hands.*

When the speed dating event ended, Keira was supposed to partake in some dancing while the organizers tabulated the yes matches, but she skipped out on that bit. She didn't feel like dancing with any Craigs or Carls, or any plumbers, Dublin based or otherwise. Because there was someone else she wanted to spend the evening dancing beside. And even though she pretended the reason she decided against collecting her list of successful matches was because she was worried that no one would have put her name down as a yes, it was really because she was only interested in one specific man's opinion of her.

*

Keira wondered, as she looked across the bar at Orin, whether this was what it was like to have a father. It was the end of the second week of her trip and the two of them were munching on their breakfast of toast, egg, and sausage; something that had become a ritual for the two of them. Since the rest of the B&B guests came and went, Keira's consistency allowed for a father-daughter friendship to blossom between them. Her own father had left while she'd still been young so she'd never had the chance to find out what that would feel like.

"Where are you and Shane off to today?" Orin asked, setting his coffee down in its saucer.

At the mention of his name, Keira felt a warm feeling spread through her. Nothing had happened between them. Not externally, anyway. Emotionally things seemed to be deepening. Their connection seemed to grow stronger every time they met. Keira found herself looking forward to seeing him each day, anticipating their next excursion with excitement. It felt like each passing day brought her further away from Zachary and pushed her closer to Shane.

Keira checked her notes. "We're going to Dingle," she said. Then looking up, she added, "Or is that a joke?" She never really knew when it came to Shane.

Orin chuckled. "There's a place called Dingle, all right. Beautiful spot. You'll love it."

Keira didn't think she'd ever get over these funny names. She'd filled her phone up with photos of street names and town signs, sending them to Bryn and Nina indiscriminately.

Just then, Keira felt her phone vibrate and checked to see she'd received an email from Joshua. She groaned to herself. His pestering was becoming unbearable. He shouldn't even be awake at this time; it would be the early hours of the morning in New York City! It must be the crazy sleep-wake schedule his painkillers were causing.

Keira, you've been in Ireland for two weeks and have sent me barely anything. Mere paragraphs. Simple sentences. Where's the story?!? I don't care how "good" Nina says your little schemes are if you can't transform it into a compelling narrative. If I could fire you and take over, I'd have this assignment done in a matter of days. You're just exploiting the fact I'm in a position where I need you to write this piece. But don't forget there's always future assignments, Keira. We'll be in that boardroom together again soon enough and once we are I will use everything in my power to get you kicked off Viatorum and never work again!!

Keira quickly stashed her phone away. She'd started to get used to these kind of abusive messages from him, and their impact was lessening somewhat. Plus, Joshua was far less scary on the other end of an email than he was in person. Not having to actually be face to face with him while receiving his verbal bashings made him far easier to ignore. But she wouldn't be able to carry on like this indefinitely. Ignoring her boss was a short-term solution to the very real and long-term problem of her having written very little of value so far. She was dreading the day he decided to actually pick up the phone to berate her. It certainly couldn't be too far in the future now...

"I should try to get some writing done before Shane arrives," Keira told Orin.

This had become another one of their rituals. Breakfast, then Keira going upstairs to "get some writing done" before heading off with Shane for another "tour of Ireland." Except really what she was doing after breakfast was sitting in her room staring at her laptop until Shane arrived to whisk her away for what was to all intents and purposes a date.

Orin nodded, accommodating as ever. Keira went up to her room.

She sat by the window, looking out at the cobbled street below and the signs of last night's party still fluttering in the wind, her laptop sitting closed on the desk beside her. For a recently dumped women who was a hair's-breadth away from getting fired she felt incredibly happy with the way her life was going.

Keira opened her document, the one that consisted of the initial rant she'd written followed by notes and unusable interviews. There was also a long passage she'd written about her heartbreak over Zachary, although she could hardly even recognize herself in the writing anymore. Those feelings had already faded away. As much as she was loath to admit it, Joshua had actually made the right call when he trashed her idea of incorporating the breakup into the piece.

Yet he was still demanding this be a personal account. Which basically meant Keira had to pretend to hate it here, to still believe that romance was dead and love just a relic of centuries gone by. But lying was easier said than done. With her fingers hovering over the keyboard, Keira just could not bring any words to mind. All she could think about were the couple who won the horse and cart race, the divorced man at the bar, Shane's parents and their everlasting affection. Romance. Love. It was everywhere. And she was falling for it.

What she really needed was to find someone lonely who she could channel when writing. Just then, Keira had a sudden moment of inspiration. Leaving her laptop behind, she rushed downstairs to find Orin. He was reading his newspaper at the bar, their empty breakfast plates still laid out in front of him.

"That was quick," he joked when he looked up and saw Keira striding toward him. "Didn't get much done, I take it?"

Keira took the bar stool opposite him. "I was wondering, actually, whether I might be able to ask you what your story is."

Orin frowned and put down his newspaper. "My story? What story?"

"Your romantic history," Keira said. "You work here alone. No wife, right?"

"So you noticed," Orin quipped.

"Well, what's the deal there?" Keira asked. "What's your story? I mean every year you get overrun by attendees to the Festival of Love. But you have nobody to love yourself."

Orin's expression became suddenly downcast; his lack of luck in love was evidently something that got him down.

Keira felt a flicker of relief to know that at least someone in this town was unlucky in love. Maybe there was still a chance to turn this all around. If she put herself into the mindset of Orin, for whom love had eluded, perhaps she'd be able to capture the voice Joshua needed from her for the article. She could play a character. At least that might ease some of the guilt she felt about having to bash this place in her article.

"I never married," Orin said, glumly. "Never found the right girl."

Keira suppressed her smile, but secretly she was filled with glee to know that she was finally getting some material.

"Was William never able to match you?" she asked.

Orin shook his head. "He tried, all right. But I'm picky, Keira. I'd meet a nice girl but then something would ruin it, something silly would start to bother me. I'd break up with her and go back to William and say, 'yes, that was close but can you make sure the next one doesn't bite her nails?' Then William would find me one that didn't bite her nails and I'd say, 'yes, close, but can you find me one that doesn't dye her hair?' On and on like that until suddenly I'm sixty and alone."

Keira nodded, keeping her expression somewhere between neutral and sympathetic. She scribbled Orin's story down in her notebook and tried to think of ways to work his narrative into the narrative she needed to create.

"So the idea of The One never came true for you," Keira pressed. "When did you decide it was never going to happen?"

Orin looked puzzled. "I haven't given up." He seemed a bit affronted by the suggestion. "I'm still holding onto hope." Then his expression became even sadder as he added, "Do you think that's foolish of me?"

Keira looked at him, torn between getting the inspiration she needed and comforting her friend. She sighed and put her notebook down. "That's not foolish. Not at all."

"You don't think that maybe love isn't for everyone?" Orin asked, a hopeful glint in his eyes. "That maybe not everyone can be happy?"

Keira shook her head and gazed at him sympathetically. "I think that William can work miracles if you just give him the chance." She realized as she said it that she actually believed it. The matchmaker's successes were everywhere. He'd made a living from it. More importantly, he'd made hundreds of people happy and content. "I think there's someone for everyone," she added. "Maybe sometimes it's just about waiting for the right moment to meet them."

Just then, the door opened and in walked Shane. Keira sat bolt upright, almost startled by his appearance at that exact moment. It felt a bit too coincidental.

He was wearing a white top with a cartoon bear on it and jeans. Simple, yet gorgeous. Keira couldn't stop herself from swooning. She'd taken to wearing a thicker foundation just to hide her blushes when he was around.

"You ready?" Shane asked Keira, strolling over and picking up a piece of discarded toast from her plate.

Keira nodded.

"Keira was just attempting to lift my spirits," Orin explained.

"Oh?" Shane asked. "Why do you need your spirits lifted?"

"Because I'm a lonely old fool," he said.

Keira felt a pang of guilt then. She should never have used Orin like that, trying to make him feel bad about his situation and lack of luck in love just for her own gains. This article was toxic for her. The whole job was. She felt like more of a fraud than ever.

She got off the stool and leaned forward, kissing Orin right in the middle of his forehead. He looked bemused.

"What was that for?" he said, blushing.

"You're not an old fool," she said. "You're a lovely, gentle man. There's someone out there for you. Just keep your mind and eyes open. You'll find her soon enough."

Orin smiled. Then Keira looped her arm through Shane's and they left the pub together.

*

"You have got to be kidding me," Keira said, laughing. She was looking at the flank of an enormous chocolate-colored horse that Shane had just informed her she was about to ride through the countryside of Dingle.

"Why not?" Shane said. "Never ridden a horse before? I thought America was home of the cowboy! Cowgirl, in your case."

Keira gave him a withering look. "I'm not from the Midwest. I'm from New York City. We're very cultured there, I'll have you know."

Shane folded his arms. "Look, if you're going to be a wimp…"

"I'm no coward!" Keira protested, rising to his bait immediately. "I can ride a horse as well as anyone. Probably."

Shane grinned to himself. "Then let me give you a leg up."

Keira exhaled, shaking her head. How did she get herself into these situations? Shane knelt down and cupped his hands over his knees for her to step into. Keira placed her foot in his makeshift stirrup and rested her hands on the horse's back.

"Ready?" he said. "On three. One, two, three."

Keira felt herself being flung up in the air. She threw her leg around, twisting until she was on the horse's back. She let out a cry of delight.

"I did it!" she exclaimed.

"Very good," Shane replied. He walked over to his own horse, a dappled gray, and quickly mounted her.

"You're a natural," Keira said.

"Of course I am," Shane replied. "I grew up on a farm. I've been riding horses my whole life."

Keira smiled, adding the talent to the list of others than Shane possessed. She found his company so exhilarating because he'd lived such a different life from her. His life had been filled with adventure, with nature. Hers had been busy streets and high-rise buildings. Not that she'd want to swap them—she'd never have survived growing up in a place like this—but she was glad their past experiences were so different. It meant they brought such different things to the table.

"Right, you follow my lead," Shane said.

He kicked his legs into the horse's flank and she began to trot forward. Keira did the same, copying him.

They took it slowly, the horses treading delicately through the fields, along paths that had been made purely by hoof. Trees stretched up either side of them, making dappled shadows skitter across the ground.

"It's really beautiful here," Keira said, breaking the silence for the first time.

"Peaceful, right?" Shane agreed. "There's nothing like a horse ride through the countryside to clear your mind."

"You need to clear your mind?" Keira asked, picking up on a hint of sadness in his tone. She wondered whether he was homesick again. Or whether he was thinking of Deidre and John.

"I meant you," Shane said, laughing.

Keira frowned, puzzled. "What makes you think I need to clear my mind?"

Shane barked out a laugh. "You're joking, right? You walk around with your head in the clouds these days. I can tell Ireland's got under your skin."

Keira felt herself blush. It was more than just Ireland that had got under her skin.

"I mean, what happened to the stressed NYC princess I met two weeks ago?" Shane continued. "You're supposed to be writing an article but you're acting like you're on vacation! No, not quite that. You're acting like one of those hippie types who spends all day meditating and doesn't need a job because they grow all their own vegetables in the garden."

Keira tutted with mock disapproval. "Hardly."

"You don't believe me?" Shane mocked. "Look in a mirror next time you're near one. You won't recognize yourself."

Keira didn't say anything. Shane was probably far closer to the truth than he realized.

They reached a small creek and the horses clopped through, splashing water as they went. Keira felt her shoes become sodden. They were an expensive pair of leather brogues but remarkably, Keira didn't care in the slightest. Soggy shoes was a small price to pay for such a magical experience, and even if the leather was ruined and stained with muck, it would remind her of this moment forever.

"So when are you going to get the guts up to ask William to match you?" Shane asked Keira.

She furrowed her brow. "You think he should?"

His question had confused her. She thought they were getting close. Had she just been seeing what she wanted to see?

"For inspiration for your article," Shane clarified. "Isn't that the whole point of being here? To see whether it works?"

"Oh," Keira said, trying not to let her relief show too much.

She considered Shane's suggestion. Maybe that was the way to go. If William matched her with someone it would inevitably be disastrous, because it was Shane she wanted. Maybe a bad date would give her enough material to put into her article. But at the same time, the thought of dating anyone made her feel odd for some reason. It would feel a bit like she was cheating on Shane, even though they weren't a couple.

"Why don't you go first?" she said, diverting attention from herself and her confusing feelings. "Go on a matchmaker date and let me take notes."

Shane just laughed. "That would be weird. And anyway, I'm not looking to date at the moment."

"You're not?" Keira asked, feeling a sinking sensation in the pit of her stomach. "Not looking for another Tessa?"

"Who?" Shane asked.

The swooping sensation of disappointment in Keira's gut grew. She remembered how Bryn had told her Shane was a player and how she'd immediately decided to ignore her advice and get close to him anyway. But he so clearly was; he couldn't even remember the names of his conquests!

"Never mind," Keira said.

They carried trotting on in silence.

"Oh crap," Shane said, suddenly.

"What?"

Shane pointed up. Keira looked to the sky. It was gray and there were clouds rolling quickly toward them.

"It's going to rain," Shane said. "Want to head back? We might need to canter."

"I can't canter!" Keira cried. "Are you crazy?"

"Either that or get wet," Shane replied.

Keira sighed. "Then I'll just have to get wet."

They turned the horses around and headed back the way they'd come, at an equally slow pace as the one they'd headed out with. In a matter of moments, the sky split open and a downpour began to drench them.

"How are you feeling about cantering now?" Shane shouted over the sound of the rain cascading off tree leaves.

Keira glared at him. She began to shiver, already soaked to the bone. The horses began tossing their manes, showering them even more. Their hooves kicked wet, sloppy mud onto their clothes.

When they reached the creek they'd passed before they found that it was now more of a river, at least a foot deep whereas before it had been merely a few inches. The water moved rapidly.

"The horses won't want to cross this," Shane shouted over the downpour.

"What do you mean?" Keira cried. She shoved tendrils of wet hair off her face.

"It's too fast. They'll bolt and then we'll be stuck."

"What are we supposed to do then?" Keira shouted over the sound of heavy rain.

"We'll just have to wait it out," Shane said.

Keira was less than impressed. Her mood worsened when she saw where Shane was directing; toward a large dilapidated barn made of rotting wood. The roof was caving in in places, letting water seep through. Only the middle part of the structure would provide them with anything even remotely resembling shelter. Warmth was definitely out of the question.

Shane helped Keira down from the horse. She landed in a muddy puddle. Then he tethered the horses up.

"Isn't that a bit cruel?" Keira asked. "Leaving them out in the rain like that?"

"They can't exactly stand there with us," Shane replied, pointing at the narrow section of roof and the dry patch beneath it. It was barely even a foot across. The horses would only be semi-covered anyway. "They have waterproof coats," he added. "It's us we should be worrying about."

He gestured for her to go inside. Keira shivered as she stepped over branches and mulch and debris from the caved in roof. This didn't seem particularly sensible, like the building could easily fall down if the wind picked up.

She stood in the dry patch, keeping her arms tightly into her body so they were out of the downpour cascading down either side of her. Now out of the rain, she became aware of how every last inch of her was wet, right down to the underwear.

"I'm never going to get my article written stuck here," she moaned.

At least she was in a bad mood again, the sort of mood Joshua needed her in for the article. If she could cling onto this feeling until she got home, maybe she'd stand a chance of writing something halfway decent. A page of whining to get him off her back.

But Keira found her mood didn't last that long at all. Because Shane was looking at her with a sparkle in his eyes.

"What?" she said. "Why are you looking at me like that?"

"I was just thinking," Shane began, "how this would be the exact moment in a romance film when the two leads kissed for the first time. The rain. The shivering damsel."

Keira felt like she'd been knocked sideways by his words, by the burning look in his eyes.

"Well, this isn't a movie," Keira said. "This is real life."

Shane took a step closer to her. "You know what they say, though, don't you?" His voice seemed to have dropped in volume.

Keira swallowed. Shane was close enough for her to see the raindrops rolling down his skin. Feel the warmth radiating from him. She looked up into his eyes.

"What do they say?" she asked, hearing her own voice sounding as husky as his.

Shane took the final step needed to close the space between them. He was now right next to her, so close their skin touched. He reached out and cupped his hand beneath her chin, tipping her head up.

"They say," he said, "That life imitates art."

93

Then he bent his head closer to her and pressed his lips against hers. Keira felt her whole body begin to burn in response. No longer was she shivering from cold. Now she was shivering from passion, from desire. It was a sensation like none she'd ever felt before.

So much for clinging onto her bad mood. Keira felt exhilarated, carefree. Happier than ever before.

CHAPTER TWELVE

There was no denying it anymore. Keira had fallen for Shane, hook, line, and sinker. Back in her room at the B&B that night, she could still feel his lips against hers. The memory of their kiss lingered on her skin, tingled in her mind. All her concerns about Shane being a player seemed to disappear entirely. What did Bryn know? She hadn't been there, she hadn't felt what Keira had felt. The emotion in that kiss was mind-blowing.

Keira felt like she was walking on air as she got herself ready for the night's festivities. She dried her hair and styled it curlier than usual. She painted her lips red, rimmed her eyes with kohl, and slicked mascara onto her lashes. It was more effort than she'd put into her appearance since she'd gotten here, and she realized with surprise that she was dressing up for Shane. She wanted to impress him, dazzle him with her beauty. She wanted to throw herself into this thing, whatever it was, and see where it led her.

She spritzed herself with perfume and skipped out of her room. When Orin saw her emerge into the pub his eyes widened.

"Have you got a date?" he asked.

Keira shrugged coyly. "Might have." She giggled.

Just then Shane came into the pub. Keira felt her whole body erupt with tingling, like electricity was flowing through her veins.

Shane walked right up to her confidently, slid his arm around her waist and pulled her close to him. He planted a deep, sumptuous kiss onto her lips. Keira felt herself melt into him, the whole world disappearing around her as her entire focus was narrowed down to the sensation of Shane's lips.

When they pulled apart Orin looked surprised. His cheeks were a little pink. But he didn't say anything, instead busying himself with pouring pints, trying to make it look as if he hadn't seen a thing.

"You look gorgeous," Shane whispered into Keira's ear, his breath tickling her skin.

"So do you," she replied with a sultry voice.

Shane kept his arm around her waist, protectively holding her close to him. Then he led her through the pub, opened the door at the end for her, and gestured her through. Keira thoroughly enjoyed the courteous gentleman routine. She loved a bit of flirty chivalry.

Out on the street, the party was already in full flow. Noisy crowds of drunken revelers wobbled past them, singing loudly, arms tangled around each other's shoulders. But Keira could hardly see them. She was completely absorbed in her own world, a world that contained nothing more than Shane and his burning gaze that made her feel naked.

They went to one of the stalls and Shane bought bottle of wine. He poured two glasses and handed one to Keira.

"I thought Irish lads didn't drink wine," Keira teased.

"Irish lads will drink anything if it will impress a beautiful lady," Shane replied.

Keira's heart fluttered at the compliment. They settled down at a table and shuffled closer, heads bowed together.

Just then, Keira became aware that the vacant seat next to Shane had become occupied. She silently chastised the inconsiderate person who'd sat right next to a couple so clearly in the throes of lust. They must be so drunk they didn't even realize they were intruding.

But then the person in the seat said something that made Keira straighten up with surprise.

"Shane?"

It was a woman's voice. Keira looked up at its owner, taking in the sight of her thick wavy blond hair, her tanned face covered in freckles, the clumpy mascara on her eyelashes. Shane glanced over his shoulder. Keira noted the way his body tensed as he identified the woman in his mind.

"Aren't you going to introduce me?" the woman added, looking at Keira with an unimpressed expression.

Keira's mind instantly went to a bad place, a paranoid place. Was this another Tessa? Another one of Shane's conquests?

"What are you doing here?" Shane said, ignoring her request to be introduced to Keira, the fact of which made Keira feel worse. Could he not remember this woman's name either? Or worse, was he choosing not to introduce Keira in order not to ruin any possible future liaison with this woman?

"I came here hoping to see you again," the woman said.

Shane folded his arms. He looked tense and uncomfortable, like two worlds that should never collide had. Keira felt herself growing hot with panic.

She stood.

"I should get back to my room," she said. "Get on with writing."

"Don't go," Shane said.

"No," Keira refused. "I need to."

She hurried off, leaving Shane with the smirking woman who looked triumphant at her success in scaring Keira away.

Feeling like a fool, Keira hurried through the cobbled streets back to the B&B. She burst through the door into the crowded pub, shoving her way past people in her haste to get upstairs.

As soon as there was no one around to see her, Keira let her tears fall. She hurried up the stairs feeling like a complete idiot for trusting Shane, for ignoring her gut instinct, for crying over another goddamn man!

She ran into her room and slammed the door, tugging off her stupid shoes, wriggling out of her slinky dress. She chucked them on the floor and stood there, panting, tears falling from her eyes, furious with herself and furious with Shane.

She wrapped herself up in her dressing gown and paced back and forth across the room. Then suddenly, for the first time in weeks, Keira felt a real spark of inspiration. She sat down at her desk, grabbed her laptop, and began to type. She directed all her hurt and rage into her fingertips. Angry, snarky words flowed out of her and onto the open document before her.

What happens in the town of love when you're a veteran? Did the matchmaker ever stop to consider the awkward encounters that may come about when old flames meet new, or when his services are used not by the lovelorn lonely but by players searching for simultaneous dating experiences? Virtual dating apps aside, there is surely no better place to procure a stream of gullible, vulnerable prey than at the matchmaker's meat market.

Keira kept on typing until her fingers were almost numb, battering the keys like a pianist playing a passionate concerto.

Then she was interrupted by the sound of a knock at the door.

"I'm busy, Orin!" she called out.

"It's Shane," came the voice on the other side.

Keira stopped typing. But only for a moment. She wasn't going to let Shane sweet talk her out of this place she'd finally found. To think she'd almost ruined her career for that stupid man! The last thing she was prepared to do now was let him in. She typed again, her fingers bashing against the keys with increased fury.

"Can you let me in?" Shane pressed. "I'd like to talk to you."

"NO!" she shouted. "Go away!"

Shane clearly wasn't about to respect her wishes. Keira heard his muffled voice come through the door again.

"Pretty please?" he said.

"I said NO!"

There was silence for a moment. Keira hoped that meant Shane had gone away. But then she heard his pitiful, pleading voice once more.

"If you're jealous about that woman or whatever then don't be. That was Caroline. My ex."

She turned angrily and thundered to the door. She unlocked it and yanked it open.

There was Shane, looking sheepish, his eyebrows raised halfway up his forehead. Even while infuriated with him Keira couldn't stop the sensations that took hold of her at the sight of his gorgeous face.

"I'm not jealous!" she yelled. "Why should I be jealous?"

"I didn't mean you should be," Shane said, backtracking. His features twisted with consideration. "I just figured you might be because you ran off when she sat down."

He scratched his neck nervously and looked at her like a lost lamb. Keira let out a grunt of annoyance at his utter cluelessness.

"Well, I'm not," Keira snapped. "Contrary to popular belief, women aren't constantly measuring themselves against each other while competing for the attention of stupid hairy … *men."*

Shane looked tickled by her comment. He pressed his lips together, clearly in an attempt to not laugh.

"Stupid hairy men like me, you mean?" he said, his usual cheekiness beginning to eke back into his tone.

"Yes. Like you."

"I see," he said, diplomatically. "So you *weren't* jealous of Caroline because you're *not* competing for my attention because I'm stupid. And hairy."

Keira pouted. "Don't mock me."

Shane pressed his lips tightly together. "I'm sorry. You're just cute when you're mad. Makes me want to make it up to you." He reached out and touched the collar of her dressing gown.

Keira jerked away and batted his hand off. "Oh, I bet it does. I bet everything makes you want to… you know. I know men like you. I know how you operate."

Shane looked mock offended. "I'm not a robot!" he said. "I don't come with an operating manual."

"You're a player!" Keira shouted. "A user. A serial one-night-stander!"

Shane burst out laughing. "What on earth are you talking about?" he said as his shoulders shook with amusement.

The sight infuriated Keira further. First he'd lured her into this trap whereby she thought she wanted him, and now he was laughing at her for figuring out the truth!

"Caroline tonight. Tessa! How many others are there, Shane?"

"Other whats? Women? Last time I checked just shy of three billion."

"Other women you've slept with!" Keira bellowed.

Shane looked bemused. Or was it amused? Keira couldn't quite tell which.

"Well," Shane began, tapping his finger. "There's Deidre, my dead wife—"

"Shane," Keira interrupted. Laying on a guilt trip about his dead wife was the last thing she wanted.

"What?" he exclaimed, still laughing but also evidently becoming exasperated. "You're talking crazy. I don't even know who this Tessa you keep going on about is!"

Keira looked at him with narrowed eyes. "Really? You really don't remember? Way to prove my point." She folded her arms. "Tessa. As in that woman you slept with on the first night of the festival"

Shane's face practically cracked from the power of his shock and amusement. He took Keira by the shoulders.

"I didn't sleep with her!" he exclaimed. "We had a drink and a flirt and a dance. That's all. If you're going to accuse me of anything then it should be my charm. Because a player is the last thing I am. Jeez, I even told you I was married once. Isn't that enough to make you realize I'm not a player? Because you know they don't usually tend to be the settling down types."

"That was years ago," she refuted. "You can change."

The fact that Shane seemed more amused than angry at her accusations made Keira feel even more stubborn. She stood there staring at him, fuming, not wanting to back down. But even while angry with him, Shane was irresistible to her. How much nicer it could be to believe him, to back down, give in. She wanted it more than anything.

"But I haven't," Shane implored her. "I've had three sexual partners in my entire life."

Keira wasn't sure whether he was down playing his sexual history to strengthen his argument. Three seemed impressively few. It was far less than she had, she realized a little guiltily. She felt herself start to back down.

As if realizing she was weakening, Shane slid his hands from her shoulders down her arms, then stopped at her hands. He took hold of them both and gave her a reassuring look.

The physical contact awakened all of Keira's senses. She felt her resolve starting to weaken.

"I really thought you'd slept with Tessa," she said.

Shane shook his head. "Nope. I'm actually very careful with my sexual partners. I don't just jump into bed with anyone. And I never have two girls on the go at once. When I like a girl, I'm all in. One hundred percent. And I'd already met you before I met Tessa so I was never going to do anything with her."

Keira felt the warmth radiating from his hands. She paused, letting his words sink in.

"Wait. What do you mean?"

Shane's smile twitched on his lips. "I mean I was already falling head over heels for you, dummy."

Keira frowned at him, unable to contemplate what he was telling her. "You hated me when we first met," she said. "You thought I was a snob. A princess. You called me Little Miss NYC."

Shane smirked. "Nah, I'm pretty sure it was you who hated me. I thought you were a babe from day one. I just wasn't going to act on it because you had a boyfriend. I was pretty bummed out about that. I thought it was just my luck to have found a sexy, smart lass like you and to find out she was already taken."

"But you went to the graveyard because you felt guilty over Tessa."

"I felt guilty over *you.*"

"Oh," Keira said, dumbstruck by his words. She didn't even know how to respond to Shane now. If this was just him sweet talking her, then boy, was he good at it! She was falling for it completely and utterly.

Their hands still clasped, Keira backed away from the doorway, taking a step back into the room, tugging Shane in with her. She noticed her laptop still open on the desk, the angry tirade up on the screen. She let go of Shane's hands and rushed over to shut it before he got a chance to see what she'd written.

By the time she turned around he was there, right in the middle of the room, just a foot away from her. It was the first time he'd been inside her bedroom and Keira felt a thrill as she saw him standing there. She felt her insides gnawing, yearning for him.

He gazed at her adoringly, his tight-fitting gray shirt showing off his physique. As if possessed, Keira found herself suddenly unable to hold back. She flung herself at him, wrapping her arms around his neck, pulling his body in close to hers, pressing her mouth against his. Shane responded with equal passion, his hands sliding beneath the cotton fabric of her dressing gown, finding her bare back and tracing his fingertips against her hips. She thrust her hands deeply into his hair, entwining her fingers in it.

They pulled apart, both panting, the gaze between them burning like fire. Then Keira's hands were on his shoulders, pushing him gently backward toward the bed, wanting him more than she'd ever wanted anyone in her life. Mouths feasting greedily upon each other, they tumbled down onto the mattress.

CHAPTER THIRTEEN

Keira awoke the next morning in a tangle of limbs. Shane was holding her close to him, cocooning her. It was cozy and comfortable.

Keira smiled to herself as she replayed their passionate lovemaking last night in her mind. It had been the most mind-blowing encounter of her life. Sex with Zach had been nice at first, then routine. She hadn't even realized how much the fire between them had fizzled until she'd been ignited by the power of Shane!

As she looked at his gorgeous sleeping form, she couldn't help but wonder about the future. Her trip wasn't going to last forever. Did that mean this amazing thing she'd found with Shane would end as well? It was unrealistic to think they'd continue dating once she returned to New York City. The flights would cost more than either of their salaries permitted, and could a relationship really exist without even occasional physical contact? The thought that there was a time limit to their lovemaking filled her with dread.

She moved then, and Shane stirred, opening one eye a sliver.

"Morning," he said, sleepily, smiling radiantly at the sight of her. He tightened his arms around her waist. "And where do you think you're going?"

Keira smiled in response. "I was going to make a pot of coffee."

Shane nodded and released her. "That's allowed."

Keira laughed and got out of bed, finding her legs wobbly somewhat beneath her. She went over to the counter where there was a kettle and a jar of instant coffee granules. It was hardly luxurious, but Keira couldn't care less. Today she was floating.

Keira made the coffee and returned to bed.

"So," Shane began, taking his mug from her hands. "Now that you know I'm not a player, does that mean we're a couple?"

Keira's eyes widened. She hadn't expected Shane to cut so quickly to the chase. But the idea didn't scare her. If anything, it thrilled her. And even though she could already imagine Bryn's reaction—telling her this was nothing more than a rebound from Zach—she didn't care. If this was how great rebounds felt then she ought to have them more often!

She tilted her head to the side and peered at Shane. "Sure."

Shane laughed. "Sure? Is that all I get?"

Keira batted her eyelids. "What would you prefer? 'Oh yes, yes, please say I can be your beloved!'"

"That's much better," Shane joked. "And yes, you may."

Keira smirked with amusement. "So what's the plan today? Where are you guiding me to?"

Shane pulled a face. "I kinda feel like it would be weird for me to act like your tour guide now. Don't you?"

"Well, my company is paying you…" Keira quipped.

"I'm pretty sure they're paying you too," Shane replied with a wry smile. "And that doesn't seem to make you do any work."

"Touché!" Keira replied.

They laughed together. Keira felt buoyant. Even the daylight filtering in through the thin curtains seemed brighter today. Not even the ever-present layer of gray clouds in the sky could bring down Keira's mood.

"Why don't we decide where we should go together, in that case," she said to Shane.

"You mean like a date? An actual date? With an activity?"

Keira nodded her head. "How about a gallery?"

"Sure. There's a ton of artists in Ireland, you know. The Limerick City Gallery of Art is closest to us. It's about an hour drive. You up for it?"

"Sounds great," Keira said.

"We'll be passing through a couple of towns with odd names that you can send pictures of to your sister."

"You've noticed me do that?" Keira asked, surprised by his attentiveness.

"I notice a lot of what you do," Shane replied.

They finished their coffee and dressed for the day. Downstairs they found that Orin had laid out a breakfast buffet for them. But Orin himself was nowhere to be seen. He must be giving them some privacy, Keira thought. Either that or he was embarrassed and avoiding them!

After a quick breakfast they headed out of the B&B, hand in hand. Shane went to walk left, Keira right. They pinged back together like an elastic band.

"The car's this way," Keira said.

Shane shook his head. "No. *My* car is that way. *Your* car is over there." He pointed the direction he'd tried to go.

"I'm not driving!" Keira stammered. "You always drive!"

"I did," Shane smirked, "when I was the tour guide. But I'm the boyfriend now. Which means we share stuff. I've never seen you drive before. Don't you think that's the sort of thing a boyfriend should experience?"

"But I'm terrible on these roads!" Keira protested. "They're too small. I'll kill us both."

"I have faith in you," Shane said.

He tugged her hand and Keira relented. The thought of driving more than she needed to in this place filled her with dread.

The rental car was parked round the side of the B&B. Keira got into the driver's seat, feeling immediately out of place.

"If I'm driving, you'll have to be official photographer," Keira said. She handed him her phone.

"No problem. I'll get pictures of Bunratty, Cratloe, and Dooradoyle's signs."

Keira laughed. "Thanks. That sounds perfect."

She turned the car on and swallowed her nerves, then reversed out of the lot.

Luckily the traffic was light.

They reached the first sign on Shane's list and he snapped a picture as they passed.

"Who am I sending this to?" he asked.

"Nina," Keira said. "It's her turn."

"No problem," Shane said.

She watched as he scrolled down to find Nina's name and sent the picture off to her.

A moment later he turned to Keira. "She replied saying Joshua is on her case about you. Can you send her some words?"

Keira sighed. But then she remembered the tirade she'd written yesterday. Was it mean to use it? She was certain Joshua would like it, and it would definitely get him off her back for a day or two. But she didn't feel that way anymore. In fact, she felt pretty much the opposite! If she sent Joshua the rant and he wanted it in the final piece then Shane would be mad if he read it. Then again, that was a lot of ifs.

"I'd better pull over and send her an update," Keira said.

"I can do it," Shane said.

Keira shook her head as she pulled up at the side of the road. "No way." She reached for her bag in the back seat and pulled out her laptop. She quickly composed an email to Nina and sent off the document. At least now she could relax.

They continued on. Keira's phone buzzed with another incoming message.

"Nina says thanks, that's brilliant," Shane told her. Then he took a photo of Cratloe's sign.

"That one's for Bryn," Keira told him.

He sent the picture off for her.

"She's replied with some emojis. The laughing cat. The laughing ghost. The smiling frog. I think we can safely assume she's amused."

They reached Limerick and pulled up into the parking lot of the gallery. Keira let out her tense breath as she parked up and turned off the engine.

"How did I do?" Keira asked. "We're both alive, which is the main thing."

Shane peered out the passenger side window as if checking to see whether she'd parked straight. "Your driving is pretty good considering," he said.

"Considering what?" Keira replied, raising an eyebrow. "That I'm a woman? Or that I'm American?"

"Your words, not mine," Shane quipped.

They got out of the car and went inside the gallery. It felt very romantic strolling around together looking at art. Keira had to keep forcing herself to focus on the paintings because her gaze kept wandering to Shane. He was the real work of art here, as far as she was concerned.

They went to the gallery's cafe and ordered some lunch. It was a cool space, open plan and modern, filled with tall plants. A glass roof let in as much light as the overcast day was giving them.

"This place is really nice," Keira said, looking around her.

Just then, the server arrived with their plates of couscous, pita bread, spicy hummus, and olives, a multicultural feast that Keira had not expected to find in the deepest depths of Ireland.

"Art is really valued over here," Shane explained. "In all its forms. Pottery. Paintings. Music."

"Yes, I had noticed the fact that everyone can play an instrument," Keira said, remembering the first time she'd clapped eyes on Shane as he stood on the stage with his fiddle. "Although I've yet to see a harpist, which I'm a little disappointed about."

"Really?" Shane asked, surprised. "I know at least ten. Remind me to take you to the Hope and Anchor on a Wednesday night. My friend Claire has a weekly spot there."

Keira smiled to herself, feeling like Shane was wanting to fully immerse her in his actual life. Not just the tourist bit but the bit with his friends.

But the more she thought about it, the heavier she felt. It wasn't like there were endless amounts of Wednesdays for them to choose from. In fact, there was just one more before she left Ireland. The likelihood of her meeting Claire the harpist was nonexistent. Because the truth of the situation was that Keira *was* a tourist. No matter what her intentions, or Shane's intentions, she would be leaving soon. The thought filled her with dread.

"You look sad," Shane said, suddenly.

Keira tensed. She hadn't meant to show her emotions on her face. She didn't see the point of them talking about the fact this was all temporary because it would just spoil things. But at the same time, her leaving soon was a fact, and they couldn't bury their heads in the sand forever.

"I'm just thinking about how we don't have much time left," she said. "You know, for me to see Claire or meet any of your friends. That sort of stuff."

"Oh, yeah," Shane said glumly. He reached across the table and squeezed her hand. "I've been thinking about that too."

She looked across the table at him. "You have? What have you been thinking specifically?"

She wanted to hear Shane's side of the situation since she'd been replaying hers in her mind over and over for days.

"I've been thinking about how much it will suck when we say goodbye," Shane said.

Goodbye. That's where Shane's mind was going. Not to long-distance dating or keeping in touch via video messaging. Not even arranging a date in the future when they could meet again. He'd gone straight to the cold, hard finality of goodbye.

"Yeah, I guess it would be unrealistic to even think about dating once I've gone," Keira said, brushing her hair behind her ear, trying to appear nonchalant when she was feeling anything but. "I mean, there's the whole Atlantic Ocean in the way."

Shane's hand on hers squeezed tighter. "Well, that didn't stop your forefathers, did it?"

Keira wasn't in the mood for a joke. She'd been getting far too wrapped up in playing boyfriends and girlfriends for her own good. But like always, Shane seemed to just be seeing the funny side.

Feeling suddenly uncomfortable, Keira removed her hand from beneath his. It was an awkward gesture that didn't go unnoticed by Shane.

"Keira, I'm saying if people crossed the Atlantic in boats, we can do it in planes. What's seven hours in this day and age? We can view the flight as an opportunity to binge watch TV shows."

But it was a little too late for his words to comfort her. Even if Shane did want this to keep going on, even if the thought of long hours airborne didn't bother him, how on earth would they afford it? Neither was particularly rich. On her current income she could probably shell out for one trip to Ireland to see him a year. It would the same, if not worse, for him.

"I don't know if even binging on TV can save this," she said glumly.

Shane looked at her with an aching look in his eyes. "You sound like you're giving up."

"No," Keira said, shaking her head. "I'm just being realistic."

"I can think of another word instead of realistic," Shane said. "How about unadventurous. Boring."

"Charming," Keira muttered.

But she knew Shane was just teasing her because he was smirking. But she just couldn't feel amused.

"Keira, we're both young enough. We shouldn't be thinking about how realistic or logical our decisions are. I'd rather spend every cent I have flying across the world to see you than save up for a *pension* or anything as boring as that. Come on, cheer up." He grinned at her encouragingly. "Let's just cross that bridge when we come to it, yeah?"

Keira could feel a lump in her throat. Though she half agreed with what Shane was saying, she couldn't help the sudden sense of finality that had taken hold of her. It had come in a wave, as if she'd left her mind behind and it had suddenly caught up with her.

Not wanting to cry in front of Shane, Keira excused herself then to use the restroom, leaving her bag with him. In the mirror, she stared at herself, wondering what she had let herself get into. On one hand it was thrilling. Throwing caution to the wind was empowering. But on the other hand she felt like she was setting herself up for a fall. That she was foolish, and had been unwise in her decision to let things progress so much with Shane. This couldn't end well, could it? Then again, nothing really lasted forever. Maybe the finiteness was part of the appeal. He'd never get a chance to see her crazy, nor she his. It could stay this close to perfect for its duration.

Steeling herself, Keira left the restroom and returned to the table. When she got back she discovered that her laptop was out on the table.

"What are you doing?" she asked, shocked, rushing toward Shane.

"I just wanted to see what you'd been writing," he replied innocently.

Keira snapped the lid shut. "Well, don't. It's private!"

"How can it be private?" he said, laughing. "You're publishing it for the world to read."

But Keira didn't see the funny side. Shane had come far too close to catching her out. It rattled her.

"Yeah, once it's been edited," Keira replied. "I don't want you seeing it in its first draft state."

It was half a lie. Though her first drafts were indeed embarrassingly awful, her main reason was because she didn't want Shane to see what she'd written. Without an explanation, and taken out of context, it would paint her in a pretty bad light. Come to think of it, even with an explanation it made her look awful.

"Besides, it's for a very specific audience. Are you an unmarried American in the twenty-four to thirty-four bracket? No? Didn't think so."

She sat down with a huff, folding her arms.

"I'm sorry," Shane said, clearly picking up on the fact he'd upset her. "I won't snoop again. I was just curious. You're always so busy I just wanted to see what with. I mean you've seen me play the fiddle but I haven't seen so much as a single sentence you've written. And you've seen me doing my tour guiding job. I'd love to see you in your reporter role."

"Maybe another time," Keira said stiffly.

They finished their food, their mood more somber than it had been when they'd come. Keira felt terribly guilty for her part in it. If she wasn't such a snake with so much to hide, Shane wouldn't have actually done anything wrong at all.

They headed back to Lisdoonvarna in the car. This time Keira kept her phone with her. The laptop incident was far too close for comfort. What if Nina messaged her an edited sentence, or some feedback on something cruel she'd said. If Shane saw her words she'd feel terrible.

They arrived back at the town and Keira parked. When they entered the B&B, they saw that Orin had finally decided to make a reappearance. He looked a bit uncomfortable as he glanced at them both, but he was as friendly as ever.

"Drinks?" he asked.

"Bit early for me," Keira said. "And I've got some edits to work on. I'll just settle in the corner with my laptop. You two go ahead."

As Orin poured a pint for himself and one for Shane, Keira increased the distance between them. She felt so terrible about double crossing everyone that it was almost unbearable to share in their revelry. Had she let herself get carried away with the whole boyfriend-girlfriend thing? When Shane was just a sexy guy she had the hots for, things were a bit more simple. At least she didn't feel like she owed him anything, like honesty. The thought turned her stomach.

Keira looked through Nina's last email, which contained edits for the piece she'd sent that morning. To her relief, it was good news. Joshua actually liked it and wanted her to carry on in that same way.

"Did he really use the word 'like'?" Keira messaged Nina.

Her reply came. "I know. I think the doctor's increased his dose of Advil though, so don't take it to heart."

Keira laughed to herself. It was nice to be in contact with Nina. It grounded her, reminded her where she'd come from and why she was here. Without her friend's dry sense of humor and regular updates Keira might have gotten even more carried away with herself than she already had.

She busied herself on her laptop in the corner as Shane and Orin drank and chatted happily.

"So, Keira," Orin called over to her. "Shane tells me you're a bit protective over your writing."

"Just the bad stuff," she called back.

She really didn't want this to be the topic of conversation again and tried her best not to rise to the bait. She was feeling bad enough as it was about what she'd sent off. But Orin, like Shane, wasn't about to drop it.

"It doesn't have to be a first draft," he suggested. "What about something that was printed in last month's magazine?"

Keira tensed. This was getting far too close for comfort. But what choice did she have? Her excuse to Shane earlier had been that she didn't want him reading anything incomplete. No first drafts. But last month's magazine had her writing in it, and the month before that. Maybe if she just pulled up the *Viatorum* website she'd be able to show them a small snippet of work. Maybe that would be enough to get them off her back.

"Fine," she relented. "Here's a piece I wrote for a parade last month. It's not very good, I must warn you."

Shane and Orin came over. They looked impressed by the website's slick design, though Keira knew that Shane at the very least would be thinking it was snooty.

Suddenly, Shane reached forward and snatched up the laptop, yanking it away from her grasp. He was giggling like it was some joke, and Keira realized as she looked up at Orin's smiling face that they had planned this. They'd ganged up on her in order to steal her laptop and see what she'd written about the festival.

"Don't!" Keira pleaded.

They had no idea. They thought this was innocent fun. They thought they were just playing with her, breaking down her modesty. But Keira knew the truth. Her stomach swirled with fear at what she knew was about to happen.

It was too late. Shane began to read aloud from the latest snarky piece she'd sent. His voice went from lilting and jovial to quiet, despondent, and deeply hurt.

"Suffocating Irish hospitality?" he read, looking up at her with sad, betrayed eyes. "Gritty, dark dive? Is that what you think of us?"

"I'm sorry," Keira whispered, her stomach sinking.

Shane looked at her with a pained expression. "What's this? Why are you being so mean?"

"It was my assignment," Keira tried to explain. "But it's not really how I feel. I'm supposed to act all snobbish for the article, that's all. It's not me. I'm sorry."

"So you're saying it doesn't count because you don't mean it?" Shane shot back, sounding upset.

"I'm so sorry," Keira repeated. It was all she could think to say. "I know it's no kind of an excuse."

"You can say that again," Shane said. "You're completely trashing us. I thought this was supposed to be a tourism magazine. What kind of tourism magazine trashes the places it reviews?"

Keira bit down on her lip. "It's less tourism and more, um, travel and lifestyle, I guess?"

"Sarcastic travel and ironic lifestyle," Shane said. "What's the point of that?"

Keira felt terrible. She shrugged. "I don't know. It's stupid. Shallow. And I've been a fool for letting myself get wrapped up in it. What can I say to make it up to you? To you both. Other than that I'm truly sorry."

Orin spoke up. "You really think sorry is enough? I put my heart and soul into this B&B. This could ruin me."

She looked over at him. He looked so disappointed in her. She felt just as disappointed in herself.

"I'm so sorry," she whispered. "I would never have done anything that I thought could hurt the business. Not that many people read the magazine. I don't think it would influence them. I mean our readers wouldn't come to a place like this in the first place." Keira snapped her mouth shut, realizing how bad what she'd just said sounded, and how the two of them were going to construe it.

Shane looked at her coolly. "A place like this?" he repeated.

Keira felt cold all over. Now she'd really blown it.

Shane downed the last dregs of his beer and swept up his coat from his stool.

"Where are you going?" Keira said, her stomach dropping with dread.

Shane kept his voice quiet. "You don't need a guide anymore. You've seen everything there is to see. I think it's best if we part ways now. You can handle this on your own."

"Shane!" Keira called out, reaching for him, feeling regretful.

It was no use. He turned and left the pub. Keira looked back at Orin. He shook his head and averted his gaze.

Keira felt as if her whole world had suddenly fallen away beneath her feet.

She ran for the door to the corridor and pulled it open, thundering upstairs to her room. Once inside, she grabbed her phone and rang Bryn.

When her sister answered, Keira let her tears fall.

"Sis," Bryn said, gently. "What's happened? Is it Shane?"

"Yes," Keira admitted. "But not just Shane. Orin too. They read my article and now they hate me."

"Isn't Orin like an old man?" Bryn said, sounding confused. "Why do you care what his opinion is?"

"Because he's my friend." Keira's chest felt heavy with guilt and shame. "I honestly don't know if I can stay here anymore. It's Orin's pub. And what's the point? I can't write anything good. Now that everyone hates me I don't see the point in staying here."

"So what if some people hate you?" Bryn challenged her. "You're not there to make friends! You're there for your career. Nothing's changed. It's just gone back to how it was when you first arrived."

"I've changed, Bryn," Keira wailed. "I don't even know how to write anymore. This is useless."

"I don't believe that," Bryn replied, refuting her claim. "You're an amazing writer, sis. Always have been. And you're a fighter. You don't run from your problems, you face them head on. Talk to Shane. Stick this out."

Keira sniffed loudly. "I thought you thought he was a player. A rebound. What do you care if I work things out with him or not?"

"I don't know," Bryn said, exhaling loudly. "It just sounds like you're having an amazing time and enjoying the company of an amazing guy. Don't let this one little thing get in the way of that. What's here for you in New York City to come back to anyway? You'll be sleeping on my couch!"

"Great," Keira huffed, pouting. "So I'm basically stuck between a rock and hard place."

"You never know what might happen," Bryn said. "Go and weave some of your word magic with Shane. I'm sure you can win him over."

But Keira wasn't quite so sure she could. She didn't think there was any coming back from this. Shane had looked so hurt. He would never forgive her. She'd ruined the one good thing she had going for her.

CHAPTER FOURTEEN

The next morning, Keira wasn't surprised when there was no breakfast waiting for her at the bar. When Shane didn't arrive to take her on an excursion, she was equally unsurprised. Her stomach twisted and turned with grief.

She knew she should attend some festival events anyway, but she felt too numb to do so. Without Shane it would just be depressing. So instead she ran back upstairs to her room and shut away the outside world.

Keira wanted to leave, to run away from this place, this whole country, and forget all about it. But there were still four days left of her trip. She knew even a pleading phone call to Heather wouldn't result in a reschedule of flights. Even if Heather herself was kind-hearted about the situation (which Keira knew she wouldn't be anyway) Joshua would veto it. He'd say something about how much she'd cost the company already. How it would be his head on the chopping block, not hers, or something equally dramatic. The last thing she wanted right now was any kind of interaction with Josh.

Keira felt at a complete loss. She wished there was some means to communicate with Shane but she didn't even have his number. If he could just give her a chance maybe they could talk this through, resolve it.

Suddenly, she remembered the itinerary Heather had given her. Josh's assistant had planned everything meticulously. Surely she'd have included Shane's number in there somewhere!

Keira searched in her bags for Heather's itinerary. She found it and scanned the document, searching for Shane's number. There it was! He was listed as "The Guide." How strange it felt now to think back on him as her tour guide, when he had become something so different, something so much more.

She felt her nerves grow as she typed his number into her phone. She listened to the phone ring, then voicemail kick in. Deliberating for a moment, Keira decided to leave a message.

"Hey, Shane, it's Keira. Can we talk?"

Her voice sounded stilted, more nervous than she would have liked. She lost her confidence and hung up before she had a chance to say any more. What she really wanted to do was apologize. Grovel. But that hadn't exactly done her any favors before and now it felt like she'd lost all her inner strength.

Her phone pinged, indicating a message. She tensed, hoping it wasn't Joshua. Praying that it was Shane. It was neither. Instead, it was a text from Nina.

I've had an idea. You need to see who the matchmaker matches you with. It would make a great concluding paragraph, don't you think?

Keira's heart sank. The thought of approaching William for a matching made her feel sick. She didn't even want to think about being with another man. She just wanted things to go back to how they'd been with Shane.

But Nina was right. She was consumed with writer's block as it was. Maybe a visit to William would give her the spark of inspiration she needed. A bad match now could provide her with the final paragraph or two for her article.

Keira wasn't quite sure how, but somehow she managed to get out of bed and out onto the streets of Lisdoonvarna. She strolled slowly to William's, biding her time. But there was only so slow she could go down the one road before she found herself outside the burnt orange house far too soon.

She took a deep breath and knocked. Maeve answered.

"Keira?" she said. "I was wondering when we'd see you."

The comment made her stomach clench. Had it really been that obvious to everyone that things with Zachary would end? Did she really appear to everyone as such a hopeless wretch that a trip to the matchmaker's would become inevitable?

She followed Maeve inside, and the flame-haired woman went off to make a pot of tea. William looked up from his desk at Keira and smiled.

"Take a seat," he said. "You're here for your match, I presume?"

Keira gave a small shrug of affirmation and sat down, filled with trepidation.

William began thumbing through his tome of names, taking his time. Maeve poured Keira a cup of tea, which she drank quietly.

Suddenly, William slammed the book shut. The verdict was in. But what he said next hurt Keira to the core.

"No match."

"I don't understand," Keira said.

"I'm unable to find someone for you. I can't match you."

"What do you mean you can't match me?" Keira said, appalled.

"Well," William began, "it's not that easy finding suitable partners. Not when I want every match to be the next Simon and Sylvia."

"Who are Simon and Sylvia?" Keira demanded, feeling insulted by William's inability to match her.

"I matched them fifty years ago at the festival," William explained. "They fell so head over heels in love they married while they were still here. They've been married ever since."

He showed her their photograph; a happy, smiling couple in black and white, beaming from ear to ear on their wedding day. She recognized William's office in the background of the photo by the cupids painted on the walls.

"They married here?" Keira asked, surprised. "Right here in your office?"

"In front of it," William explained. "They come back to Lisdoonvarna most years to catch up and for a celebration."

Keira handed him back the photo. "Well, I'm not looking for a husband," she contested. "I just want a date. For inspiration. For my article. Surely you can do that?"

William looked less than impressed by her admission. He folded his arms. "That is a misuse of my services," he told her.

Keira left William's office feeling frustrated, her ego bruised. Typical, she thought, that even the matchmaker couldn't find anyone for her. She must be a leper or something.

The only good to come out of the whole thing was that when Keira sat down to write that evening, she managed to write two whole bitter pages on the topic of being unmatchable. Nina loved it. Even Joshua seemed quite keen on it, though Keira had to wonder whether his good mood was to do with his painkillers. Either that or he took great pleasure in her misery. Keira concluded it was more likely to be the latter.

CHAPTER FIFTEEN

When Keira's penultimate day in Lisdoonvarna arrived, she awoke with a heavy heart. It was hard to believe that her plane was tomorrow, that the month was almost over, and that she would soon be returning to New York City. She wasn't sure how well she would cope with all the high-rises and queues of taxis after the quaint quietness of Ireland.

As she showered and dressed for her final full day, William's story about the happily married couple replayed in her mind. Maybe if she could track down Simon and Sylvia somehow, and hear their side of the story, she'd have the last bits of information needed for her article. Because there just had to be more to it than love at first sight and fifty years of wedded bliss. She refused to believe it worked that way, that it could really be that easy.

The problem was, Keira only had her memory of a photo taken fifty years earlier to rely on in finding them.

She checked all the usual haunts, the pubs, the corner shops. Everyone she spoke to either knew Simon and Sylvia personally or knew of them. But no one seemed to know whether they'd come this year. And whenever she asked for their contact details she was met with suspicion.

The woman in the pub next door to Orin's seemed to know Simon and Sylvia well. But she wouldn't help Keira.

"You're the reporter, aren't you? The American?" she asked, accusingly, folding her arms.

"Yes," Keira admitted with a sigh. She was getting used to people distrusting her now. Word had spread quickly about the piece she'd written and how she'd bashed them all in it. Friendly faces were much harder to come by these days.

"Then I'm not telling you anything. I know what you're like. You'll twist it for your piece."

Keira left the pub with a heavy heart.

Despite her failure, she didn't much feel like returning to the St. Paddy's Inn. Orin was still barely saying two words to her. So instead she found herself wandering along the street without direction.

Right on the outskirts of town she found a small patch of grass she'd not noticed before. There was a sign proclaiming that it was a park, the smallest in Ireland, which Keira could believe because it was only about as long and wide as a bus. There was a solitary tree, a bench, and a statue of the Virgin Mary. Keira sunk down into the bench. As she did so, her eyes skimmed over the little gold plaque affixed to it.

Simon & Sylvia.

She couldn't believe it. The Lovers of Lisdoonvarna had built their own park with their own bench and own tree. It was absurdly romantic.

Keira decided that all she had to do then was stay here on the bench and wait for the two of them to arrive. They were certain to do so at some point. She just had to be patient. It wasn't like she had anywhere else to be.

She waited and waited, at times feeling foolish, at others Zenlike in her ability to remain patient. The air grew cooler as the daylight began to fade. Soon people were streaming along the road, filing out of their hotels and B&Bs for the night of festivities. But Keira stayed put. She'd heard enough of their stories. It was Simon and Sylvia's she wanted now, so certain was she that theirs would be the one she needed to finally finish her piece.

She must have fallen asleep at some point because Keira suddenly became aware of two faces peering down at her. She startled up to sitting, her back twinging. How long had she been lying on the hard bench snoozing?

Keira realized then that the two people looking at her—an old man and woman—were familiar. They were the elderly couple she'd seen at the horse and cart race, back when she and Shane had still been on good terms, before she'd ruined everything with him, forcing herself to receive yet another bruise to her heart, so close to the one Zach had caused.

"You're not Simon and Sylvia, are you?" Keira asked.

The man and woman looked at each other.

"That we are," Simon replied, smiling. "We must be famous, Sylvs, if they know about us on the other side of the pond."

The woman chuckled. "It's about time. You know I've always wanted to appear on *Oprah*."

"I was looking for you," Keira said. "I'm a reporter, writing an article on the Festival of Love. And you're the golden couple, the big success story."

Sylvia seemed to brighten even more when she said that. "We really are famous, Si!"

"Can I ask you some questions?" Keira said.

"Please do."

They sat either side of her, sandwiching her between them. It was uncomfortable to say the least.

Keira got her notebook and pen out. Then she paused.

"Full disclosure," she said. "The article I'm writing isn't the most complimentary of pieces."

Simon frowned then, confused. "Why ever not?"

"Oh no," Sylvia added. "She's a cynic."

Simon looked sad for her. "Breaks my heart how these young people behave these days. No one has any faith in each other. No one sticks relationships out anymore. They think it's all about the lust and passion. But that only carries you through the first few years. Then the work begins."

Keira began jotting down his words. "So you've found your marriage hard work?"

Sylvia laughed at that. "Goodness no! Not hard. Work, yes. But work is rewarding. I'm sure you'd agree with that."

Keira wasn't so sure anymore. She'd found this whole experience grueling and tiring. But she still cared more about her career than her love life.

"I guess," she admitted.

"And even when it is hard," Simon continued, "you don't mind because you want it to work. You're both striving for the same thing, for success in your marriage."

Keira noted down the way the two seemed to share each other's thoughts, one beginning a train of thought while the other finished it. It was as if that'd been together so long they'd forgotten where one of them ended and the other began.

"I suppose I'm most interested in these tough bits," Keira said. "You've both mentioned having to work at the relationship. What's been difficult for you?"

"Most things," Sylvia said, her eyes sparkling with amusement. "There's been a great deal of compromise. Should we paint the kitchen green or blue? Should we invite his mother over for Christmas or mine?"

"You must have had more disagreements than that," Keira said. It sounded rather petty to her. "Sylvia, tell me, did you have to choose between motherhood and a career?"

"Oh yes," the woman said. "For a while, when the children were very young and needed me around. I was a nurse, you see. But when you get to my age and look back on all the years you've had, a five-year career pause doesn't seem like that much of a big thing. Hardly a sacrifice at all."

Keira scribbled down the story. She looked at Simon. "Did you appreciate the sacrifice Sylvia made in order to bring your children into the world?"

"Of course!" he exclaimed. "Our children mean the world to me, to both of us."

"Simon sacrificed too, during that time," Sylvia added. "He had to work doubly hard at work to support the family. We both had to make concessions for what we wanted."

Keira tried to see the negatives in their story, to read the bad between the lines, but they were just so damn likeable. They shared a kind of calm demeanor that must have come about through years of patience and compromise.

She folded the cover of her notebook back. "Do you think you're both better people for having found one another?" she asked.

She wasn't asking for the article anymore, but for herself, for her own curiosity. She'd always felt like settling down was giving in. Committing forever to one person was akin to giving up on yourself. But she was starting to consider a different possibility; that being united with a lover in marriage made both parties stronger, better, nicer. There was power in unity. She'd simply never realized before.

Simon and Sylvia smiled at each other.

"We certainly do," they both said.

Keira could see the love and adoration in their eyes as they gazed at each other. She'd seen it before, in Calum's and Eve's eyes when they looked at each other. And in the couple who'd won the horse and cart race, the Polish woman and her newfound beau.

There was another place she'd seen it, and that was in Shane's eyes when he looked at her. Had she been teetering on finding true love only to ruin it by prioritizing her snarky article? Had she done the thing Zach always accused her of, of giving more of herself to Joshua than to their relationship?

"I need some advice," Keira suddenly blurted.

"Go ahead," Simon said. "We've become something of agony aunts over the years, haven't we, Sylvs?"

The woman nodded her agreement.

"I think I found someone," Keira explained. "Someone really decent. But I hurt his feelings. I said some mean things."

"Have you apologized yet?" Simon asked. "That word sorry goes a long, long way. It's one of the greatest lessons you learn in marriage; that even when you're certain you're right, you are often wrong!"

"I haven't had the chance," Keira said, glumly. "He's ignoring me. I haven't seen him since the fight."

"Have you called?" Sylvia asked.

"He never picks up," she said. "And even if he did, I have no idea what I could say to him to get him to forgive me."

"Be honest," Simon said. "Speak from the heart. If your intentions are pure, he'll be able to see that. Whether he acts on it or not is a different matter, and not something we can answer for you. But if you give him every chance to forgive you then you'll be able to sleep easier knowing you've done everything in your power to make amends."

Keira looked from Simon to Sylvia and back again. Their sage advice rang in her ears. There was no way she was going to add them into her article. They were the real deal. And more than at any point during her whole trip to Ireland, she realized that she truly did believe in love. Not just as something that could happen, not as a compromise made through fear of loneliness, but as a pure, beautiful thing to be nurtured, cherished, and tended to like a garden.

Keira stood up from the bench, suddenly filled with motivation.

"Thank you, guys," she said. She went to rush back to the St. Paddy's Inn, but turned around quickly and added, "Happy anniversary!"

As they waved goodbye, Keira hurried away, finding herself filled with renewed energy and focus. Because she wanted what they had. She wanted the silver anniversary, the gold. She wanted the compromise and sacrifice. The respect and patience. She wanted to grow and experience all that love, true love, had to offer. And she knew who she wanted to experience that with. She just had to convince him of the same!

CHAPTER SIXTEEN

As Keira hurried back to the inn, she heard her phone ringing in her bag. She grabbed it, wondering if Shane was finally calling her back, as if they were telepathically connected somehow. Instead, it was Joshua's name that she saw flashing on the screen at her.

So he'd finally decided to shout at her. His dose of painkillers from the broken leg must have been reduced.

Sucking in her breath, Keira answered the call.

"Tick tock, Keira," Joshua said menacingly, not even bothering to say hello. "You're nowhere near finished. Where's my final draft? I need to see how it all hangs together with the disastrous date the matchmaker sent you on."

Simon and Sylvia's advice was still ringing in Keira's ears. She made a decision there and then. No longer would she pander to Joshua's demands. She wasn't feeling it, the article would be phony. She needed to write from her heart, speak her truth. She was going to delete everything she'd written so far and start again. She was going to write something she actually *cared* about. She was going to drop the irony, the snark, the condescending arrogance. Because this place had taught her something far more important. The power of love.

"I didn't get to go on one, remember? He refused to match me." She smiled to herself as she said it, realizing what William had been doing when he failed to match her. He'd been stopping her from falling into the same dating traps she always had, from wasting her time on unsuitable people. He really did know what he was doing and Keira was finally willing to accept it.

"Then how are you ending the piece?" Joshua yelled, sounding incensed.

"Don't worry. I have something else up my sleeve that will blow your mind."

She was certain it would do just that. Just not in the way that Joshua was expecting.

"Tell me what it is first," he demanded. "I want to make sure you're heading in the right direction."

"I just met a couple who got married here," Keira said. "The Lovers of Lisdoonvarna, they call them."

"Okay. And? What's the problem? Are they both hideously ugly? Ex-cons? What's the deal? How are you going to spin it?"

Keira suppressed a smile. "Let's just say they had some interesting anecdotes and some advice for a young woman."

"Which was...?" Joshua prompted. He didn't sound like he was buying it.

Just then Keira reached the B&B. "Look, do you want me to write this piece or chat about it? Because I know where my efforts would be best expended."

Joshua let out an infuriated cry. "Fine, Swanson. Do what you want. You always have. God, if I could go back in time and unspill that macchiato, unbreak my leg, I would make sure you NEVER got this piece. You've been nothing but trouble. I've had to micromanage this whole thing from my bed!"

Keira just rolled her eyes. She'd heard enough of Joshua's angry tirades.

She finally got to hang up the phone and entered the busy pub. Orin was behind the bar, as usual. He looked up, then back away again when he saw her enter. Keira had taken to scuttling away from him, ashamed, hiding up in her room. But this time she walked confidently up to the bar.

"What can I get for you?" Orin asked, looking surprised that Keira was standing in front of him.

"I wanted to apologize," Keira said, emboldened by Simon and Sylvia's words earlier. "I'm so sorry about what I wrote. I was trying to get approval from all the wrong people, like my boss back in New York City. But I've come to realize that doing things to make bad people like you is akin to being a bad person yourself."

Orin watched her intently as if letting her words sink in. Keira felt happier with every second that passed. Apologizing, admitting guilt, it was cathartic.

"I wanted you to be the first to know that I'm not going to publish the article," she continued. "I'm going to withdraw it. My editor has the most recent draft, she's a friend. I'm going to ask her to delete her copy so my boss can't get hold of it. It will be completely erased, everything I said."

Orin frowned then. "What are you going to do instead? It's still your job."

"I don't care," Keira said, and to her surprise she realized that she meant it. She really didn't care. She didn't want to write pointless ranty articles just to impress Joshua. "Even if it costs me my job I'd prefer your friendship and respect over Joshua's any day!"

Orin suddenly smiled. He came out from around the bar and hugged her tightly. Keira felt that surge of fatherly love again that she'd lost when she'd broken Orin's trust.

"I'm so happy to hear this, Keira," Orin said. Then he released her from the embrace. "But you know who really needs your apology? Someone who is probably living in hope that you'll have a change of heart before you leave?"

"Shane," Keira finished for him.

Orin nodded. "Shane. You should call him."

Keira chewed her lip, thinking of the message she'd left on Shane's voicemail. It had been inadequate. She'd hardly even broached an apology.

"I know," she admitted. "But I left a message and he didn't return my call. I don't think Shane wants to hear me groveling."

Orin looked at her sternly. "One voicemail? You're giving up after one knock back?"

"I don't want to seem like a stalker," Keira said.

"Would you prefer to risk being perceived as uncaring instead? Because that might be how you come across."

Orin was right. One voicemail was pathetic. She had to show Shane how much she cared. And she was running out of time to do it.

CHAPTER SEVENTEEN

Up in her room, Keira held her phone in her trembling hand and tried to calm her ragged breath. She dialed Shane's number, willing him to pick up, to stop blocking her out. But he didn't. The voicemail clicked on.

"Shane, it's me again. I know you don't want to speak to me but hear me out, please? There's so much I need to say. I know there's nothing I can say to make this okay. And I understand if you don't accept my apology. But I really care about you, Shane. And I'm leaving tomorrow. I don't want us to part like this, on this sour note. I need you to know how sorry I am. I wish I could go back in time and not write a single one of those awful words. I was wrong. I was being the snob you thought I was. But everything has changed now. Please, let's talk this through. I don't want to go without saying a proper goodbye."

She hung up. Leaving the message had been very difficult to do. But hadn't Simon and Sylvia told her the best course of action was honesty? She sounded nervous because she was, and there was nothing wrong with Shane knowing that.

She sat on the bed and stared at her phone, breathing deeply. She'd never felt so on edge; not when Zachary was losing it that day when she told him she was flying to Ireland; not even when Joshua had called her out and insulted her in front of the entire writing staff. She realized now that that was because she hadn't cared about either of those things even half as much as she thought she did. What she cared about was Shane. How had it taken her so long to realize? To accept her feelings toward him? She'd pretty much left it until the very last second! If Shane didn't call her back today it would be too late—she was flying home tomorrow; there would be no other chance to make amends.

She twiddled her fingers and watched her phone, willing it to ring. Then suddenly it did.

Keira's heart leapt into her throat. She grabbed the phone. But it wasn't Shane calling her back. It was Zachary.

Keira felt immediately enraged to see his name there. How dare he be calling her?

She was about to reject the call—neither wanting to hear Zach's voice or block up the line in case Shane did decide to call her back—but paused for a brief moment of reflection. Why would Zachary be calling her? Things had ended so sourly between them. For him to get in touch after all these weeks of silence worried her.

Maybe it was something to do with the apartment they rented together? What if it was something even worse like his mom or sister being struck down with an illness? What if he'd been diagnosed with something terminal?

Realizing she was just going to work herself up into a frenzy by speculating, Keira reluctantly accepted the call.

"I didn't think you were going to pick up," Zach said.

It was so strange to hear his voice again.

"I wasn't sure I was going to," Keira replied. "Your voice isn't exactly one I've been wanting to hear."

"That's a bit harsh," Zach said.

"Is it?" Keira challenged him. "Were you really expecting me to be cordial after the way you treated me?"

Zach sighed. "I'm not calling you to drag up the past."

"I'm sure you aren't!" Keira said. "It paints you in a pretty bad light if I recall." She found that she was suddenly fuming. All the anger she'd had inside of her all this time was suddenly spilling out.

"Keira, can you just shut up for a minute?" Zach said. "I need to talk to you."

Keira was about to lay into him for his rudeness, but the tone of his voice concerned her. "What's happened? Is everything okay?"

Her mind went into overdrive imagining all the bad things he might be about to tell her. As much as she hated Ruth, she still didn't like the thought of her dying suddenly in a car crash.

"Yeah. It's just, well, you're coming home tomorrow, aren't you?"

He sounded nervous. Keira wondered why.

"I'm landing midday local time. But don't worry, I won't come to the apartment if that's weird. I can stay at Bryn's for a bit then arrange a time to pick up my stuff."

There was silence on the other end of the line. Then Zach spoke again.

"That's the thing, Keira," he said. "I'm wondering whether it would be too hasty for you to pack up and move out. I mean, we haven't had a post-breakup meeting or anything."

Keira frowned, confused. "Is this some new modern relationship thing I don't know about?" she asked sarcastically. "I wasn't aware it was customary to meet face to face once you'd broken up."

"I just think it would be a good idea. I mean, things can be said over the phone in the heat of the moment that shouldn't have been."

Keira grew even more puzzled. "Are you referring to anything specific?"

Another long pause.

"I just mean how are we supposed to know it's really over when you've been away for a whole month? We haven't seen each other, or even spoken really. We might feel differently when we're face to face."

"I don't think I'm going to feel differently about you cheating on me," she scoffed. "On second thought, I might feel angrier about it if I see you face to face. It will make the mental pictures easier to imagine."

"Keira, please," Zach said. "This is difficult for me."

"What's difficult?" Keira demanded, exasperated. "You're not saying anything."

"I'm being quite clear," Zach said.

"No you're not!" She couldn't help but think of the advice Simon and Sylvia had given her about apologizing, accepting your flaws, realizing you're often wrong, speaking honestly and from the heart. Zach seemed incapable of all of those things.

"I'm saying we should try again," he said finally. "See how we go. You come back to the apartment and we'll have a drink together, you know? Talk things through face to face."

Keira's frown intensified. "You mean get back together?" She could hardly believe what she was hearing. This seemed completely out of the blue.

"Sure," Zach replied. "Maybe."

His evasiveness was grating on her. He couldn't even say a straight "yes" because that would be a roundabout way of admitting he'd been wrong in the first place. Not that it would make a difference to her. She was so over Zach. This call was nothing more than confirmation of what she already knew.

"Why the hell would I want to do that?" she said. "Why would you, come to think of it? I'm never going to be the kind of girl you need me to be. You know, lacking ambition. Putting your needs above my own."

"That's not what I wanted you to be," Zachary snapped. "I was always very supportive of your career."

Keira couldn't help herself from barking out a laugh. "Yeah, because giving someone an ultimatum between taking an amazing opportunity at work and staying in a relationship with them are the actions of a completely supportive boyfriend?"

"Now you're just being facetious. There was never an ultimatum."

Keira threw her arms up, exasperated. Zachary seemed to possess the ability to rewrite history whenever he desired to support whatever position he needed it to. It was beyond infuriating.

"I think I know what's happened," Keira said. "Your little fling with Julia has ended and you're wondering where you're going to get your next kicks from. Well, listen to me carefully. It won't be with me."

"You're being crass. This isn't just about sex. What we had was great."

There he went again, reinventing the past.

"Maybe for you it was," Keira said sternly. "But it wasn't for me."

"Look, here's what I propose," Zach said, as if he just wasn't hearing what she was saying. "I'll pick you up from the airport. We'll grab coffee and lunch. Talk things through like grown-ups."

She took a deep breath. "Zach, that's not going to happen. You're literally the last person I want to see when I get back to New York City."

"Now you're being dramatic," he argued. "Let's just see how it goes when we're together again. I'm sure there will still be sparks."

"You're not listening to me!" Keira yelled, the last semblance of patience she had left completely evaporating. "I DO NOT want to be with you anymore. I DO NOT want to see you or speak to you or have a goddamn coffee with you. Because I DO NOT love you."

"I'm not asking you to love me," Zach replied. "It's not like love ever entered into the equation before."

"Then what's the point?" Keira cried, realizing as she said it just how much she now meant it. "Why bother being with someone who doesn't move your whole world?"

Shane's face materialized in her mind's eye as she spoke the words. Her longing for him intensified.

"Because we had fun," Zach replied. He was talking more quickly now, his nerves audible in his voice. Perhaps it was finally sinking in.

"That's the thing," Keira said. "We didn't have a great time together. In fact, we were pretty incompatible. If you don't love someone after two years together you're never going to, and that's not because love's changed in the modern world, it's because... it's because we just didn't have it. I'm sorry, Zach. But I know that now."

"I don't understand," Zachary replied. "You've been abroad for a month and, what, you've found yourself? That's a bit cliché, don't you think?"

Keira realized how little she cared about his criticism. Keeping Zachary happy wasn't even on her radar anymore.

"Maybe to you," she said. "But I don't care. It is what it is. I've changed. And we're over. You and me. For good."

Zach didn't seem to be getting the message. "How about I give you a couple of days to settle back into New York City life?" he suggested, sounding hopeful.

"NO!" Keira cried. "Listen to me. I'm saying no. I don't love you. I never did. I never will. I'm in love with someone else."

The words tumbled from her mouth, and she left it hanging open, shocked and surprised to hear herself. But it was true, wasn't it? She loved Shane. That's what she'd discovered since coming here. Love *was* real, because she'd found it in him.

"Who?" Zach demanded.

"No one you know."

"Someone in *Ireland*?" His tone had changed. She could hear the sneer in his voice. "That's a bit doomed, don't you think?"

Keira shrugged and took a deep breath. "I guess it is." There was nothing left to say. Loving Shane but not being able to be with him didn't equate to returning to Zachary. It never would. "I'm going to go now. Bye, Zach."

She hung up before she could hear his response.

Sitting back down on the bed, Keira stared at her phone in her hand again. But she was done willing it to ring. She'd had enough of sitting impassively in her room waiting for Shane to take the bait. She'd just admitted to herself that she loved him. There was no way she could just sit here and hope he decided to get back in touch. She was running out of time. He needed to know. And she needed to tell him.

She stood and exited her room, then hurried down the stairs. In the pub, she waved to Orin behind the bar.

"He's gone home, hasn't he?" she asked him. "To his mom and dad's?"

Orin's face twisted with indecision. "He told me not to tell you."

Ouch. That stung. But Keira was determined.

"You didn't tell me," she said. "I worked it out myself. You just nodded."

Orin looked from left to right as though checking for witnesses. Then he nodded his head quickly.

Keira smiled at him, triumphant. Then she hurried out of the pub, armed with everything she needed: a destination, a goal, and a pounding heart.

CHAPTER EIGHTEEN

Keira clutched the steering wheel of her rental car in her hands. She could only vaguely remember where she was going from the funny town name signs, remembering how Shane had sent photos to Bryn and Nina for her, how they'd laughed together that day. Was she behaving like a crazy person, driving somewhere she'd only been once to turn up on the doorstep of a man she'd known for less than a month to confess her love for him! Yep, it sounded pretty crazy in her head. If only Bryn could see her now.

It was midday and Keira realized she hadn't eaten any lunch and had no way to procure any for the next few hours. But she didn't care. She could forgo sustenance.

The drive seemed to take forever. All the adrenaline coursing through her body didn't help, since it had the effect of making time seem to pass slower. She checked her phone periodically, hoping that Shane would call her back and ease at least some of the tension she was feeling about him rejecting her. But he didn't. She ruminated on whether he'd listened to her most recent voicemail, what he thought about it if he had. Did he hate her? Would he be less than impressed—or even offended—when she turned up at his house like a possessed woman? But then she remembered Simon and Sylvia, their advice, their words, their love. That's what kept her going. All her memories of the festival converged together in her mind, each one another step that had taken her closer to this place, turning her more and more into a hopeless romantic.

It took her four hours total before she found herself on the road she recognized, the main street in Shane's town. She remembered the jokes he'd made about the different locations in the town. The "post office." The "nightclub." Doris the donkey. Her heart skipped with anticipation.

She craned her head, searching for the single track dirt road that led to the family's farm. Everything looked the same here—roads that were little more than muddy grooves made by tractor tires. Then suddenly she spotted it. She wasn't sure at all what made her know this was the road she was looking for since it looked exactly the same as the last three she'd passed, but something inside her told her this was it, she'd found it.

She yanked the steering wheel left, the car stuttering in protest as she failed to kick it down a gear into first. Consequently, she found herself thundering along the road at an uncomfortably fast pace.

Up ahead she saw something blocking the path. She just had time to slam the brakes on. The car ground to a halt behind a whole crowd of sheep.

Keira jerked forward, her chest straining against the seat belt, then thunked back against her seat. She felt the car stall, then everything fell silent.

She took a moment to check herself, to breathe and make sure nothing was broken—the car or herself. Confident that everything was indeed still in one piece, Keira glanced out the windshield at the backsides of a hundred sheep. There was no way through.

Without wasting a second to contemplate her next move, Keira threw the door open and leapt out the car, abandoning it in the middle of the path. She had to inch up against the hedges to squeeze alongside the sheep, who seemed to move like a slow-flowing river. The smell was less than pleasant, and the sheep didn't seem pleased by her intrusion. Keira had never realized quite how menacing sheep looked close up. They stared at her cautiously, and she couldn't help but imagine that they were sizing her up. She gulped and continued to shove her way past them.

Soon she found herself in the middle of the group. Everywhere she looked there was white wool, so much of it she couldn't even see below her waist. She could feel the pellets of sheep poo squelching beneath her feet, however.

At last she saw light at the end of the tunnel. She was just about near the front of the herd. She used her arms to help her wade through the crowd, like she was trying to propel herself through water. Then suddenly she was out. She wasted no time and ran the rest of the path toward the farmhouse.

When she made it to the house at the end, she was panting from the exertion. Sweat clung to her skin. The smell of sheep poo had followed her all the way, and she looked down to see her jeans covered in it, saturated up to the ankles. But even though she knew she looked like something that had crawled out of a swamp, she wasn't deterred.

She catapulted herself at the door of the farm house and began to knock.

The door flung open. There stood Hannah. Her eyes widened as she took in the sight of Keira.

"Keira?" she gasped. "Is that you?"

Keira took a deep breath, still trying to catch it from her sprint here. All she could do was nod.

"What happened to you?" Hannah cried.

Keira was only able to manage the word "sheep." She jerked her thumb out behind her.

"Oh no," Hannah said, looking up the path. "The sheep escaped again." She looked over her shoulder, back into the cottage. "Dad! The sheep escaped!"

Keira waved her arms, trying to get Hannah's attention back. There were far more important things at stake than escaped sheep!

"Shane," she managed to stammer. "Is he here?"

Hannah paused and looked at her suspiciously. "Maybe…"

Keira finally managed to straighten up, the painful stitch in her side abating.

"Can you tell him I'm here?" Keira asked. "Hannah, please? I messed up, I know that. But I really need to talk to him."

Hannah folded her arms, trying to look menacing. She was far too cute for that, though Keira wasn't about to tell her.

"I'll see," she said through pursed lips. "But I'm not promising anything."

She shut the door, leaving Keira on the porch steps. Keira listened through the door, hearing the commotion from the other side, the sound of Shane's excited sisters talking rapidly.

The door flew open again and there was Calum, dressed in boots, with the family's sheep dog at his feet.

"Hi, Keira," he said, smiling broadly. "I'm just off to deal with an escaped sheep problem."

Then he hurried off down the path. Keira looked through the open door and saw Shane's six sisters standing in the bright, warm corridor, huddled conspiratorially together, talking quickly.

"But Shane said he didn't want to see her," Neala was saying.

"That was in the heat of the moment," Mary countered. "He'll change his mind when he finds out she drove all this way for him."

"We should at least tell him she's here," Elaine agreed.

"But you saw how furious he was when he got her voicemail," Siobhan added.

Keira felt bad listening in on them like this. She coughed in order to announce her presence. The sisters spun round, alarmed to see her standing outside on the doorstep.

"Sorry," Keira said shrugging. "Your dad had to sort out the sheep situation. He left the door open."

All six sisters stared at her. It was Neala who finally spoke.

"Keira, I think you should probably go," she said. "Shane doesn't want to see you."

But then Hannah interrupted. "Girls, we should give her a chance. Don't you think?"

There was a moment where the sisters exchanged glances with each other, biting their lips in deliberation. Then, at last, they relented.

"I suppose it's up to him," Aisling said with a shrug.

Hannah looked thrilled as she ran off to fetch Shane. Keira felt her stomach twist into knots at the thought of seeing him again after how badly it had ended between them.

Then suddenly he was there, standing at the top of the stairs.

Seeing him again sent bolts of desire racing through Keira. Her mouth became dry, her palms sweaty, and she could feel her heart beating more rapidly in her chest, thudding against her rib cage.

Shane surveyed the scene below him, looking down at the huddle of women watching him expectantly from the bottom of the staircase. Keira desperately wished she didn't have an audience for this moment. It was awkward enough as it was.

Shane began to walk slowly down the stairs toward her. "What are you doing here, Keira?"

Keira looked from one sister's face to the next. They were all watching her like hawks.

"Can we go somewhere private to talk?" she asked.

Shane reached the bottom step and folded his arms. "I don't think there's anything left to say. I think you covered everything in your article."

"Oh there is," Keira exclaimed. "Trust me. There is so much to say."

Shane paused and took a deep breath. "Fine. Girls, could you leave us be?"

The sisters looked at each other, visibly disappointed to be being shut out of the drama. But they followed his command and filed out of the corridor, into the kitchen, shutting the door softly behind them. Though they'd left, Keira fully expected them to be crowding together on the other side of the door in order to listen in on the conversation, so it wasn't like they'd be missing out entirely.

With the kitchen door shut, Keira turned her full attention to Shane. He raised an eyebrow.

"Well?"

Keira swallowed her nerves. "I'm not using the article. It's not me, it's not what I think. I was trying to impress the wrong person. But I know what's important now."

Shane folded his arms. "Which is?"

Keira let the words tumble out of her, the truth, the sheer insanity of her feelings for him. "You, Shane," she stammered.

"You and me. Everything's changed since I came here, I was just too stubborn to realize. I didn't want it to be true."

"Didn't want what to be true?"

"The fact I was falling in love with you."

Shane's eyebrows raised up his head. Keira tensed. This was the bravest she'd ever been in her life, much more so than the time she'd volunteered for this position in Elliot's meeting. It was terrifying and exhilarating in equal parts.

"You *love* me?" Shane said, sounding shocked and in disbelief.

Keira threw her arms out wide in a shrugging gesture of resignation. "Yup. And I'm leaving tomorrow. I didn't want to go without you knowing. And since you weren't returning my calls, I decided to come here to tell you."

Things weren't going how Keira hoped they would. Shane wasn't throwing his arms around her nor bestowing her with kisses. He hadn't cracked a smile or teased her. The cheeky lad she'd fallen for hadn't returned at all.

Shane sniffed. "What's that smell?"

"I think it's me," Keira confessed. "The sheep escaped and blocked the road. I had to fight my way past them." She looked down at her stained jeans and felt her cheeks flush with embarrassment.

She looked back up at Shane hopefully. For the first time he let his cold exterior crack slightly, an amused half-smile flickering across his lips. But he quickly suppressed it.

"I've got to say," he began, "that fighting through a blockade of sheep is probably the most unique way anyone's ever confessed their love for me."

"Unique in a good way?" Keira asked tentatively.

Shane's smile started to take hold. He seemed to have suddenly stopped fighting it. Then his body started to shake with chuckles. Soon, he was laughing loudly and uncontrollably. Despite herself, Keira joined in. Shane's laughter had always been infectious and in this tense moment it was more so than ever.

"Yes," he finally said. "Unique in a good way."

He took a step towards her, then touched her arm lightly. Keira felt sparks ignite inside of her.

She looked up into his eyes. "Am I forgiven?"

Shane cupped her chin in his palm. He nodded. Then he brought his lips down to meet hers.

Keira gave in to her emotion. She sank into Shane, filled with relief and love and regret for having almost messed everything up so spectacularly.

Suddenly, the kitchen door burst open and out tumbled Shane's sisters. They rushed at Keira and Shane, laughing and cheering, bundling them both into a hug.

"I'm so glad you're back," Hannah squealed. "You should have seen how miserable Shane's been the last couple of days."

"I can assure you I've been just as miserable," Keira said to Shane's sweetest, youngest sister.

Neala grabbed Keira's hand. "Come on, let's have a drink to celebrate."

She dragged Keira into the kitchen, the others following, merry and bouncing.

"I can't drink," Keira said, shaking her head. "I have to drive back."

"You can stay here," Hannah said. "Can't she, Shane?"

Shane's eyes widened and his face turned pink. Keira jumped in, saving him from the embarrassment of answering such an unintentionally personal question.

"I can't stay. My flight home is tomorrow so I need to be back at the B&B."

"Even if you're driving you can have one drink," Aisling said. "Go on!"

"Girls!" Shane snapped. "Keira doesn't want to drink. Don't force her to."

Everyone around the table fell silent. Keira looked across at Shane. Tears were sparkling in his eyes.

"What's wrong?" she asked.

Shane looked around at his sisters. Almost as if they'd communicated telepathically the girls seemed to understand that he wanted them to leave. Keira felt a horrible feeling in the pit of her stomach that whatever Shane was about to tell her was going to be bad.

She watched his sisters go, desperately willing them not to, as if their presence here could stop Shane from saying whatever it was on his mind that was causing his expression to look so suddenly downcast

As soon as they were gone, he exhaled. "What's wrong is it's the last night of the festival. You're going home tomorrow."

Keira stood there, suddenly cold. She felt crushed, like she was in an elevator plummeting to the ground floor.

"What are you saying?" she whispered, feeling tears choking her, lodging painfully in her throat. "I thought I was forgiven. I thought we were back on."

Shane looked at her with a grief-filled expression. "You are forgiven. But it's too late. We're out of time."

CHAPTER NINETEEN

The drive back to Lisdoonvarna was a heart-wrenching affair for Keira. She kept playing over in her head the meeting with Shane, feeling uncertain and confused. She felt like he'd given up on her, like he'd fallen at the first hurdle. Or was she just reading into the situation what she wanted? Maybe Shane hadn't had the heart to break it to her that he didn't feel the same way and had just used her flight home tomorrow as an excuse. He hadn't said the exact words, "I love you," after all.

The darkening sky matched Keira's mood. As she drove along the winding streets, her heart grew heavier and heavier. She wished she hadn't left it so long to act on her feelings for Shane. And she wished she'd thrown out the article as soon as she'd started falling for him. She'd set herself up to fail, set their relationship a trap that was only ever going to be walked right into. She'd messed it all up, left it too late. In some ways the closeness was more unbearable than if Shane had flat out refused her.

She reached the outskirts of Lisdoonvarna to find the streets filled with people. It was the last day of the festival and people were clearly up for making the most out of it. She briefly toyed with the idea of honking her horn to force them to move, but there were so many people it would be futile. Instead, she slowed her car and crawled along behind them, feeling like she'd replaced her wooly sheep blockade with a tipsy human one. It was just her luck that when all she wanted to do was get into bed and hide she was surrounded by people.

People started to knock on her window and cheer at her, singing songs in their drunken joy. Keira felt the absolute opposite. While their festival had ended in love and romance, hers had ended in heartbreak.

She inched along the road, moving at a snail's pace. No one seemed in a hurry to get anywhere. She passed the troubadour and a group of people dancing around him, then inched past a stall selling street food. She realized as she went how much she would miss this place. It wasn't just Shane she'd fallen in love with, it was Ireland. The thought of returning to New York City filled her with dread.

As she reached the main road, she saw that huge banners had been strung up across the street announcing the final dance of the festival. It was an all-night party. Keira realized with a groan that she would be kept up all night and she knew from experience that sleep deprivation would make her black mood even worse.

She noticed in the small cobbled town square that there was a stage set up, with a sparkly backdrop and two red velvet thrones. A microphone stood in the middle of the stage, and a large crowd of people were clustered together in front of it, clutching drinks in their hands and looking expectant. Keira saw there was a sign at the top of the stage. It read: Mr. Lisdoonvarna and The Queen of the Burren. She frowned, confused.

Just then, everyone in front of the stage erupted into applause, and a huge crowd of people surged forward, stopping Keira in her tracks. She was completely surrounded. There was literally no way through. Her car had been entirely blocked in, as if it were just another spectator to whatever was about to go down on the stage.

She sighed, resigned, and wound down her window. May as well hear what was going on, she reasoned.

To her surprise, it was William who took to the stage. He had smartened up for the occasion in a shimmery suit. The crowd started chanting, "Matchmaker! Matchmaker!" William waved humbly, like a celebrity in front of dedicated fans. He was carrying his huge matchmaker's book. Behind him, his flame-haired receptionist, Maeve, followed him onto the stage. She looked like a glamorous assistant in a sparkling emerald dress.

William walked up to the microphone. "It is the moment you have all been waiting for!" he called out. "The announcement of this year's most eligible bachelors, the crowning of Mr. Lisdoonvarna and the Queen of the Burren."

Everyone clapped loudly.

"As always, we have crowns for the winners of his coveted prize," William continued.

Behind him, Maeve produced a velvet cushion with two crowns set on the top.

"Without further ado, I will now announce the winners."

Maeve handed him a gold envelope. William opened it.

"This year's Queen of the Burren is.... Keira Swanson!"

The crowd began to clap. Keira froze in her seat. There had to be some kind of mistake. She hadn't even entered the competition! Was William playing with her?

When people began to catch on to the fact that the crowned winner was sitting in her car in the middle of the crowd, they started to turn and chant, cheering her on. Keira shook her head. The last thing she wanted was to be dragged up on stage. She was still covered in sheep poo!

But the crowd wasn't backing down. And now William was calling to her as well.

Maeve took the microphone. "Keira, if you don't come up here for your crown we'll just come down there and put it on you!"

Feeling like she had no choice, Keira reluctantly unclipped her seatbelt and got out of the car. Everyone cheered and made way for her to make it to the stage. People she'd never met before clapped her on the shoulder and congratulated her. Keira felt worse than ever to know so many people wanted this crown and yet she was the one getting it.

She made it onto the stage and Maeve hugged her. Then William did too. He took the microphone again.

"For those of you who haven't met Miss Swanson, she is a reporter from New York City. When she first got here, she was cynical about love, the festival, romance in general. I hope this crown will go some way in helping her change her mind."

Maeve placed the crown on Keira's head. Little did William know just how much she'd really changed.

"Now it's time to announce Mr. Lisdoonvarna," William said into the microphone. "Now this is someone many of you will know. I've been wanting to crown him for years but never found the correct lady to match him with. That is, until Keira came along."

Keira had a horrible feeling she knew just where this was going. He was going to announce Orin, the bar man, the man she saw as a father figure. This was going to be an embarrassing moment of humiliation, a punishment for the article and her snooty attitude. William must have been planning this since day one! No doubt Orin was in on it as well. She pouted, bracing herself for the humiliation, knowing that the crowd would get a great kick out of laughing at her expense.

"This year's Mr. Lisdoonvarna is, of course, everyone's favorite tour guide… Shane Lawder!"

Keira let her mouth fall open with surprise. She turned to William, frowning.

"What?" she demanded.

William patted the book. "I matched you two on day one," he said.

Keira's eyes widened. "Why didn't you tell me!" she exclaimed.

"You had a boyfriend. And a lot of learning to do." William smiled.

Keira couldn't believe it. Would things have been different for her and Shane if William had let them in on his secret? It felt like just another kick in the teeth, another moment of too little too late.

"Shane isn't here," she told William sadly. "He went back home."

Just then, Maeve pointed out into the crowd. "No, he didn't!" she exclaimed.

Keira looked out over the rows of people and saw him, Shane, working his way through the crowd. People were urging him on, pushing him forward. Just a few feet behind her own surrounded car she noticed Shane's. He'd followed her here?

Her heart leapt into her mouth. Was this really happening?

Shane fought to the front of the stage and was given a helpful shove from the people around him. When he stood up, he raced toward Keira and pulled her into an embrace, lifting her off her feet and twirling her around in a circle.

"What are you doing here?" Keira cried.

He set her down on her feet and looked deeply into her eyes. "My sisters convinced me I was being an idiot. That I was wasting the last night we had together. They told me that even if it was only one night we had left we should make the most of it."

Keira gazed adoringly into his eyes. Then they kissed passionately. The crowd roared with pleasure.

Maeve plopped Shane's crown onto his head. He laughed, holding it in place with one hand, while his focus remained solely on Keira. She lost herself in the moment, feeling like there was no one in the world watching them, feeling like it was just her and Shane in this beautiful moment, holding on to the present day and making the most of it while it lasted.

CHAPTER TWENTY

Keira and Shane lost themselves in the music. They danced like it was their last night on earth.

"Would you like some wine?" Shane asked.

But Keira shook her head. She didn't want fuzzy memories of this evening. She wanted to remember every second in sharp clarity. Plus, she was drunk enough on love as it was.

"I do want a picture though," Keira said.

She'd been so busy taking pictures of signs of strange town names and sheep's behinds she realized she hadn't taken any photographs of the things that mattered, like Shane, and Orin, and William. That's what she wanted to preserve from her time here, the people, their faces, not a bunch of comical photographs.

"Here," Shane said, taking her camera. He tapped the man dancing next to him on the shoulder. "Could you take a picture of us?"

The man agreed and Keira posed next to Shane. Just as the flash went off on the camera, Shane grabbed her and planted a huge, wet smacker on her lips. When he released her, Keira burst out laughing and smacked him.

"I want a proper one!" she cried. "One where I can see your gorgeous face." Then to the man who'd taken it, she asked, "Another, please!"

This time Shane put his arm around her and posed properly. When the man handed back her camera, Keira looked at the two pictures. Both filled her with such joy. In the first Shane's cheeky spirit was captured perfectly. That he'd caught her off guard with his sneaky kiss attack seemed very apt to Keira, representing so perfectly the way he'd knocked her off her feet with his love. In the second picture they both looked so happy and loved up, it looked like they were a real couple. Keira didn't quite recognize herself in the photo. She'd never looked so happy before.

"I want a million pictures," Keira said. "A whole album's worth to make up for the time we lost. In as many locations as possible."

Shane seemed excited by the challenge. He clasped her hand and led her through the crowds to Orin's pub. They took several pictures with the bar man. Then Shane joined the band of musicians playing folk songs in the corner and played along with them on the fiddle. Keira snapped photo after photo, her insides feeling all gooey at the sight of her man on stage like that. She never thought anyone could make the fiddle look sexy and yet somehow Shane managed it.

Shane finished the song and leapt back down, sweeping Keira up in his arms.

"Where next?" he asked.

"William's," Keira replied.

They hurried off, hand in hand, running down the cobbled streets.

"It's a full moon," Shane said. "Let's get a selfie."

Laughing, they both stopped in the middle of the street and turned so that the moon was hanging perfectly between them. Then they snapped a photo before running off in the direction of William's.

As they went, Keira realized that she had truly become one of them. Before, she'd been sitting in her room in the B&B looking down at people like her and Shane with disdain. She realized now that it had actually been jealousy. She'd wanted what they had all along but couldn't admit it to herself. It was easier to lie to herself and pretend she looked down on them, when all along she was filled with envy. Now that she was on the other side she felt carefree, filled with joy.

They made it to William's office and took pictures of the cupids on the walls outside, pulling silly poses. In one, Keira made it look as though she were cradling a cupid like a baby. In another, Shane mimicked the arrow-shooting pose of another. The results were hilarious.

They knocked on William's door. After a while it opened and Maeve was there. She was still dressed in her emerald dress from the ceremony. With her flame red hair she looked every inch the Irish beauty.

"Maeve!" Keira cried. "We need a photo of you."

"Oh," she said, looking surprised. "Sure."

She posed with them beside the matchmaker's book. Then William himself arrived back, clearly weary from the party and ready for bed. He looked surprised to see Shane and Keira in his office.

"I'm leaving tomorrow," Keira told him. "And I'm trying to take as many photos as possible. I don't want to forget anything or anyone."

William obliged, posing for photos in his shimmery suit.

"Be sure to send me one for my wall of fame," he said with a wink as they left.

Back out in the street, Shane and Keira joined back in with the party. They danced to the music, held one another, and kissed. When they found Keira's rental car still abandoned amongst the crowds of happy people they laughed in delight and took a series of photos clambering all over it. Then Shane pulled her up onto the roof and they danced together. It was the most joyous Keira had ever felt.

So high was she from the emotion, she didn't even feel tired, which made it far easier to lose track of the time. When the sun started to rise it took her by surprise. Time was running out on their adventure.

She turned to Shane, suddenly serious. "I need to know what happens," she said. "When I wake up tomorrow and get my plane. Will we see each other again?"

"Of course," Shane said, holding her by the tops of her arms. "Our story doesn't end here. I promise you."

He seemed genuine. But had he even considered the practicalities? They'd be taking the concept of a long-distance relationship to the extreme. It wasn't like either of them was on a pop star's income.

"So you'll visit me?" she asked.

"If you'll visit me," Shane replied.

"Of course I will!" Keira said. "Especially once you're back home. Being force fed tea and cake by your amazing family is my idea of heaven."

Shane laughed. "We're going to be okay, Keira," he said. "Trust me."

Keira nodded, hiding the sober mood that was creeping into her. It wasn't that she didn't trust Shane, she just didn't think he'd really thought this through like she had. But she didn't want to end the night on heavy stuff, on practicalities and logic. She wanted things to stay magical. In a few hours (and despite their best efforts to keep things going) it could very well all be over for her and Shane. She wasn't about to let the whirlwind romance end on a low.

"There's one more place we need to get pictures of," Keira said, trying not to focus too much on the fact that their time was wearing down.

"Where?" Shane asked with a frown.

She smiled and grabbed his hand. She pulled him along the streets and back to the B&B, then led him up the stairs into her room. Shane raised an eyebrow as she gestured toward the bed.

"Don't worry, these ones are just for my private collection," Keira said with a wink.

*

Keira and Shane didn't get much sleep, not wanting to waste any of their precious time together. But there was no denying the fact that the sun was rising, making Keira's room become brighter and brighter. Each hour that passed brought them closer to the end.

At seven in the morning, Keira started to feel reality sinking in. She was going home in just a few hours. Which meant she needed to pack. Looking at her suitcase brought a wave of grief crashing over her.

"Don't do that," Shane said when he saw her tugging it onto the bed.

"I have to."

"Why don't you stay a bit longer?"

Keira shook her head. "I can't. The flights are all booked."

"Then miss them."

She looked at him sadly. "I can't. The company paid. I won't be able to afford to fly home otherwise."

Shane sat down on the side of the bed. "Then don't fly home. Stay here."

Keira couldn't believe what she was hearing. "You mean with you?" she said. The temptation was great. But she was too realistic for that. "And do what? Work on the farm with your parents?" She shook her head. "You know it can't work like that. Not every day can be a twenty-four-hour party, Shane."

He reached out for her and pulled her onto his lap, rocking her gently. "I know," he sighed.

They stayed like that for a long time.

"Can I escort you to the airport at least?" Shane asked.

"Sure," Keira said, touched by his gesture.

She finished packing and took a few last photographs of the room, then headed downstairs. Orin had prepared them a breakfast. Keira smiled, touched.

"Eat with us," she said.

Orin shook his head. "No, no, you two should have your privacy."

"I insist," Keira said.

She missed their old routine of eating breakfast together. It had been a while since they'd done so and she wanted one more fond memory to add to her collection.

Orin relented, and the three of them ate a hearty breakfast.

"How about a Guinness for the road?" Keira suggested.

Orin and Shane cheered.

Breakfast seemed to whiz by and soon Keira saw that it was time to head to the airport. She hugged Orin tightly goodbye.

"Don't give up on the matchmaker," she told him as she squeezed him. "There'll be someone out there for you and he'll know who she is when he sees her. Okay?"

Orin smiled and nodded. Shane carried her case through the pub and out the door, heading for the car. Keira followed, waving goodbye to Orin as she went.

Out on the streets, she looked at the now familiar sight before her; the road, stretching left and right, the fields ahead, the row of colored houses, and the very last stragglers left over from the night before. She was going to miss this place. She took in a deep breath of the luxuriously oxygenated air, letting it fill her.

Her car was still abandoned in the middle of the road. She watched Shane load up her cases in the trunk. His own car was parked further down the road. He'd have to catch a taxi home after dropping her off. Somehow, that thought made her even more morose.

She walked up to the car and placed a hand on Shane's back. He turned and smiled at her sadly, then slammed down the trunk door. They got into the car that only a few hours earlier they'd been dancing upon the top of. But now it wasn't a stage for their love, it was a vehicle about to tear them apart.

Keira started the engine and drove along the streets slowly, through the debris from the night before, weaving carefully around people who were still dancing. She wished she could still be one of them but soon the party would be over for them as well. She wondered how many people would be returning to a whole new life, one touched by love, or how many were going back to the same old life they'd escaped only briefly.

It was the brightest day Keira had seen so far in Ireland, which gave her the opportunity to glimpse a new side of the place. The clear sun made the scenery even more beautiful.

"I'm going to miss trees," she said, wistfully. "And sheep."

"I'm going to miss you," Shane replied, looking at her with longing.

Keira gave him a sad, half-smile. "I'm going to miss you too."

*

The Shannon airport was bustling with tourists, many of whom sported slogan T-shirts showing shamrocks, leprechauns, and harps.

Keira wondered if they'd only experienced the touristy side of Ireland, the one she'd been anticipating when she arrived and had assumed that was all there was to it. She hoped they'd at least stepped away from the tourist trappings to experience the majesty of the place.

Through the window in the lounge, rows of planes sat waiting to take people away. Soon she would be on one of them, cutting through the sky, leaving this place. Leaving Shane.

Keira saw the NYC flight flash up on the departures board.

"That's me," she said to Shane.

His face drained of color. He took her hands and brought them up to his mouth. He pressed a kiss onto each of them.

"Will you text me when you get home?" he said. "So I know you're safe."

Keira nodded, touched to see his protective side showing through. Her stomach roiled with emotion. She swallowed it all down, not wanting to make a scene here in front of all these people. Then she remembered Simon and Sylvia's advice to be true to herself, to be honest. She threw her arms around Shane and kissed him passionately, not caring that they had an audience.

"I love you," she whispered.

Shane squeezed her hand as she started to back away. "I love you too," he said.

She turned before he had a chance to see the tears fall from her eyes and strolled down the tunnel to the plane.

As soon as she was onboard she couldn't hold back anymore. She openly wept.

CHAPTER TWENTY ONE

Keira pushed open the door to *Viatorum* magazine and strolled across the tiled floors. The whiteness and glass seemed so clinical to her now, almost blinding in their brightness. The open-plan office seemed like an enormous waste of space.

All the staff looked up as she entered. There were some new faces amongst them, and some people who'd been there before who were now missing. Lisa was nowhere to be seen. Neither was Duncan. So Joshua had still been hiring and firing while on bed rest, it seemed.

Wobbling in her now out-of-practice stilettos, Keira strode right up to Nina's desk.

"You're back," Nina said, leaping up and hugging her friend. She looked over Keira's shoulder. "FYI, Joshua is coming in today for the first time since he broke his leg. Specifically to read your piece. And shout, probably. I think he's been feeling quite emasculated since being in the hospital and there are some new junior writers he needs to intimidate."

"I'd expect no less from him," Keira quipped. "Now, about the article..."

Nina narrowed her eyes. "Don't tell me you haven't finished it."

"Oh, I've finished," Keira said. "But I don't want you to publish it."

Nina exhaled, sounding frustrated. "Why not?"

"Because it sucks," Keira said boldly. "The whole thing. The brief. The assignment. I don't want my name on a trash piece like that."

Nina rubbed her face, exasperated. "And what am I supposed to do?"

Keira grinned. "I've written a new one."

She handed Nina the printed document. She'd spent the entire flight from Shannon to New York writing it, finding it far easier to write than anything she ever had before. She watched on expectantly as Nina skimmed it.

"This reads like a love letter," she said finally, looking up at Keira with a frown.

"Because it is," Keira said. "What do you think?"

"Joshua won't like it," Nina said simply.

"I know," Keira said. "I don't care about him. Do you?"

Nina didn't seem convinced. "I mean it would be better once it's been through a round of editing…" she said.

Keira laughed. "Of course, that goes without saying," she joked.

"But there isn't time because your deadline is today," Nina said, sounding more stern, letting the light-hearted jokes fall by the wayside. "And now you're telling me I have nothing to publish."

"Oh, but we do," Keira said. "We're publishing it anyway. I have a plan. But I'll need your help."

Nina folded her arms. "I don't like the sound of this."

"It's simple," Keira said, feeling mischievous. "You just *accidentally* upload the wrong draft; i.e., this one instead of the one Josh is about to read. You up for it?"

Nina said nothing for a while. Then a wicked smile spread across her lips.

"Okay. I'm in."

Just then the doors opened and in hobbled Joshua on crutches. The sense of tension increased in the office. Clearly he hadn't told any of the staff he'd be in today.

Joshua had gone to the effort of styling his quiff and had even put on a suit jacket—a lurid mustard yellow color—even though he was wearing loose-fitting jogging shorts on his bottom half. The cast around his leg went all the way up to his thigh. Keira noticed that no one had signed it, a thought that filled her with pity instead of glee.

"Keira. Nina. My office. Now."

Joshua used his crutches to hop into his office. Keira flashed Nina a confident smile and they walked across the open-plan office, all eyes on them, and followed him inside.

The second they were inside, Joshua launched right into his attack.

"I have to say, Keira, I've been appalled by your conduct during this assignment. I was counting on you to relieve my stress during my sick leave period but really all you've done is compound it. Elliot's been on my case from dawn until dusk because of you. I wish he'd never handed the piece to you. I'd have written a better article from my sickbed."

Keira listened, not rising to his insults. It amazed her how little Joshua's opinion mattered to her anymore. Her experiences in Ireland had changed her.

"And Nina's had to fit herself to your schedule as well," he continued. "It's not like you're the only writer she edits for. Do you have any idea how difficult it is for her to juggle all her commitments? I thought you two were supposed to be friends." Then with a sarcastic sneer he added, "Nice way to treat your friends."

Keira stood there taking it, letting the words bounce right off her.

"Well?" Joshua demanded. "What have you got to say for yourself?"

She handed him her article, the old one compiled of her snarky reviews. "Here's the final draft."

Joshua's frown deepened. He'd clearly wanted her to start groveling. Keira wondered if he'd even expected her to hand him a finished product at all. It seemed to have taken him off guard.

"Right," he said. He sat down heavily in one of the seats and began to read. As he did, he made occasional grunts that Keira took to be approving. Once he was done, he looked up. "It's fine. It will do. Nina, over to you now."

Then he stood.

If Keira had still cared about his opinion, this response would have devastated her. She was a junior writer after all, and this was her first big assignment. Putting all the other stuff aside—the slowness, the reluctance, the avoiding emails, which she could accept weren't good ways to behave—Joshua should still give her feedback on her actual writing. But clearly he didn't care about building her confidence or offering advice for her so she could develop her skills and improve. All he wanted to do was tear people down and reduce the competition. It was all so clear to her now. Even if she'd behaved like the Golden Girl she was supposed to, churning out scathing reviews, staying up every night to meet her impossible deadlines, he'd still have found a way to crush her spirit.

Nina took the document from Joshua.

"Thanks. Want me to run the final draft through Elliot?"

Joshua shook his head. "No, he won't be interested. He's moved on to other things now, other assignments. I'm sure he's quite forgotten about this one by now."

Keira rolled her eyes as Joshua shuffled out of the room. She caught Nina's eye and grinned.

The two went back to Nina's desk. Keira sat beside her and watched as she uploaded the new piece, the love letter to Ireland, onto the most recent issue's proforma.

Keira watched her move things around, setting the article out across a four-page spread. It looked beautiful with the addition of the photographs Keira had wanted to be included. She'd never seen her own writing appear like that. It looked real, professional. She felt a surge of pride.

"When does this go to print?" Keira asked.

Nina swiveled in her chair to face her. "Overnight," she said. "The e-zine goes live at midnight."

Keira smiled, excited for the fallout that would ensue tomorrow morning once Joshua realized just what she'd done.

CHAPTER TWENTY TWO

With no apartment of her own to return to, Keira had no choice but to go to Bryn's after work that night. She took the elevator up to her sister's apartment, dragging her still packed luggage behind her. She was utterly exhausted from lack of sleep over the last day, and all the writing she'd done on the plane. But when Bryn opened the door, smiling brightly, Keira instantly felt herself perk up.

"Sis!" Bryn cried. "I've missed you so much!"

The two sisters hugged. Keira felt so grateful to be back in her sister's company.

Bryn ushered Keira inside and led her to the kitchen. There was a bottle of wine and two glasses waiting on the counter for them. Bryn poured them both a glass and hopped onto a stool.

"Tell me everything. The time difference has been a bitch. And then you haven't replied to any of my texts or calls for like forty-eight hours. I was starting to worry your plane had gone down or something."

Keira raised an eyebrow. She'd forgotten how loud Bryn's voice could be. How many words seemed to tumble from her mouth before she took a breath. She'd become entirely unaccustomed to the pace of New York City life.

"I'm here, alive," she said. "I was just a bit busy." She smiled to herself as her memories of Shane replayed in her mind.

Bryn looked at her suspiciously. "Busy doing what? Or should I say *who?*"

Keira tsked aloud at her sister's crassness. "If you must know, I was with Shane."

"Still?" Bryn exclaimed, eyes widening.

"It was more than just a hookup," Keira said. "It was a whirlwind love affair."

"You mean lust affair," Bryn said. "Don't you? I mean no one can fall in love that quickly."

Keira just shrugged. "I met people who fell in love at first sight. People who married within twenty-four hours of meeting. There's really no right or wrong way to do love. When you find it, you find it."

Bryn looked unimpressed. "But he lives in Ireland, sis. You're never going to see him again. And the novelty of FaceTime will wear off soon enough."

Keira herself had to admit that Bryn had a point. Things with Shane had been left in the air. The sensible part of her kept telling her that nothing would ever come of it, that what they had existed in just that one point and one location in time, that she should be happy to have even had the chance to experience it. But the wild, romantic side of her that had been unleashed by the encounter wanted something different. It didn't want to let go, give up, or rest. It wanted to fight for love.

Bryn took a big swig of her wine. "What's the deal with you and Zach, then? Are you moving out? Because I mean you can stay here as long as you want, honestly, but also you know how particular I am and how much I need my me time, you know? I mean work is insane at the moment and I'm hardly getting any sleep so it's like super important that things are chill at home. I checked with Mom and she said it's cool to stay with her if you need to."

Keira looked at her sister and sighed. As much as she loved Bryn, she couldn't help but wish her sister could be a little more supportive like the Lawder girls. She realized then how much she missed not just Shane, but his family too.

"I just need to be in New York City for work while I'm finishing up the article," Keira explained. "But I have a feeling that won't take too long. I'll be out of your hair soon enough."

She smiled to herself, looking up at the clock and counting down the minutes until the piece went live. Instead of scared, she found herself feeling excited. It was thrilling to know she'd rebelled against Joshua. And unlike the trash piece she'd written before, she was proud of this one. She couldn't wait for Shane, Orin, William, Maeve, the Lawders—all the people she'd met and grown to love in Ireland—to read it.

*

Bryn's couch was so uncomfortable to sleep on, and the noise coming from the streets below so unrelenting, that Keira was almost relieved when she woke the next morning and remembered she was surely going to be fired today. She checked her phone and saw a message from Nina that had come in early in the morning saying the piece was live. Keira grinned to herself, knowing there was no going back now.

She grabbed a shower and drained a black coffee, then headed out onto the busy streets of New York City. The sheer volume of noise assaulted her, and she couldn't help but feel affected by all the miserable faces of the people hurrying past her on their way to work. She missed the tranquility of Ireland, the quiet, the happiness of its people.

She took a cab to work and went inside, seeing that she was the first to arrive. Nina came in next.

"Have you heard from Joshua?" Keira asked.

Nina shook her head. "Not yet. His painkiller schedule tends to knock him out for the night though. I think he'll be waking up around about now." She checked her watch and nodded. "So I'll give it another five minutes before he realizes what you've done."

They sat tight, waiting for the inevitable call, for the explosion that would be Joshua when he found out.

"We're getting some interesting stats on the website, by the way," Nina told Keira. She led her to her computer and logged on. "Your article's received about five times the amount of commentary we'd usually expect from our center piece."

Keira raised an eyebrow. "Is that a good thing or a bad thing?"

"Traffic is always a good thing," Nina said. Then she clicked on the first comment. It was a gushing response to the article. "But you're getting a lot of positive feedback too."

Keira smiled to herself. "I wasn't expecting that," she said. "I thought it would be far too earnest for our readers. Aren't they all supposed to be ironic?"

"Maybe Josh has misjudged them," Nina said. Then she swiveled in her chair and looked up at Keira. "Or maybe irony is just a bit passé now. I think being genuine might be the next big trend."

Keira laughed. Just then they heard the doors swing open behind them. A handful of scared-looking junior writers scuttled in.

"Poor kids," Nina said. "This is their first day with Joshua in the office. He sent a mass email round last night saying he was going to whip the magazine back into shape, that they'd disappointed him while he'd been on sick leave by slacking off. He said he'd fire anyone who came in late."

Keira rolled her eyes, remembering the level of fear he'd instilled in her at the beginning. He really was a piece of work.

Nina's phone began to ring.

"And so it begins," she said.

She picked it up. Keira could hear Joshua's angry voice buzzing through the earpiece. Nina winced and held it an inch away from her ear.

"I did what?" she said, innocently, feigning ignorance. "The wrong piece? What do you mean?" She winked at Keira then tapped some keys on her keyboard. "Oh my goodness, you're right. Boy, do I feel like a fool now. Pull the piece? Are you sure? It's getting a lot of hits." She paused as Joshua's voice buzzed through. "No problem. You're the boss. See you soon." She hung up.

"Well? What did he say?" Keira asked, on tenterhooks.

"He's in a cab. He'll be here in five minutes. If your piece hasn't been taken down by the time he arrives he's going to, and I quote, 'make someone suffer.'"

"Cool," Keira joked.

Right on time, Joshua arrived five minutes later. He bombarded his way through the doors, his face red with fury. The new junior writers seemed to shrink in their seats, all averting their eyes and tapping at their keyboards feverishly to look as busy as possible. But Joshua wasn't interested in them at all.

"Keira. Nina. My office. Now!"

His voice echoed across the room.

"Show time," Keira whispered to Nina.

They headed into the office. Joshua was pacing up and down the room on his crutches, a sight that Keira found more amusing than intimidating.

"What the hell is going on?" he barked. "What is this crap?" He waved one of the newly pressed magazines in his hand. "A love letter to Ireland?"

"I don't know what happened," Keira lied. "I must have sent the wrong document to Nina."

Joshua glared at her. "Do you know how much money you're going to cost this company? We've already printed the magazines. Half of them have already been distributed. Not to mention the website. Thousands of people have already read this drivel."

Keira raised an eyebrow. "Thousands?" she said with an innocent voice. "That sounds like a lot considering it's only been live a few hours."

Joshua's face grew even redder. "I don't think you understand the gravity of this situation, Keira. You've put the entire reputation of this magazine at stake!"

The volume of his voice was rising. Keira knew what that meant. He wanted his junior writers to hear him humiliate her.

"Plus," Joshua continued, "Heather sent me through some paperwork from your trip. The rental car company has charged us for damage to the vehicle. They said it was covered in sheep manure amongst other things. And how the hell did you manage to dent the roof?"

Keira smiled to herself as she remembered standing on top of the car with Shane, enjoying a beautiful, romantic moment. Just the memory of Shane's love felt like a protective shield around her.

"There might have been a couple of incidents," Keira replied nonchalantly. "Involving sheep."

Joshua threw his arms into the air with an angry exclamation. "Swanson, I've never been so disappointed in a writer before. You've brought shame to *Viatorum* magazine." His eyes sparkled with glee as he uttered his favorite words in the world. "Keira, you're fired."

"Why am I not surprised?" Keira shot back. She folded her arms and glared at Joshua. She suddenly realized that he didn't intimidate her at all anymore. She didn't care about his approval. In fact, him disliking her so much as to fire her caused a huge wave of relief to wash over her. She didn't want someone like Josh to like her. She didn't want to try to fit into his toxic version of the corporate environment.

"Do you know what you are, Joshua?" Keira continued. "You're a coward. You tear people down just so there's less competition. Nothing is ever good enough for you because all you're trying to do is crush people's spirits. It's how you've even gotten this far, isn't it? You just bully everyone around you until you're the last man standing!"

Through the meeting room's glass partition Keira could see people's heads craning around to see what was happening. They looked drawn and terrified. She remembered being one of them not that long ago, of watching with fear as Joshua humiliated and fired a staff writer just to prove a point. She remembered the way they'd just taken it, hadn't stood up for themselves. Well, not her. She was going to give Josh a piece of her mind.

Nina stood then. "If you're firing Keira then I quit."

"What?" Joshua yelled, incensed.

"It was as much my mistake as hers," Nina said calmly. "I was the one who uploaded the wrong piece. I should have double-checked it before I sent it off to the printer, before I uploaded it. I was slacking off."

Joshua looked at her incredulously. "That's not happening. I refuse to accept your resignation."

Keira smirked to herself. She wondered if anyone had ever quit on Josh before. He must have been so used to people fawning over him, pandering to his every whim, that to have someone throw it in his face must have been extremely unsettling.

Just then, they heard the sound of someone entering the office. They all turned and looked over to see Elliot towering over them. Heather hovered just behind him holding a black folder against her chest.

"Ladies, I'm sure it goes without saying that neither of you are fired," he said. "Joshua, on the other hand, pack your stuff and go."

Joshua faltered. He looked at Keira, confused, then back at Elliot. "I'm sorry, what did you say?"

"I've reconsidered your position here," Elliot stated in a matter-of-fact voice. "I think you were close to steering this magazine toward disaster, and it's only thanks to Keira here that we've corrected our course. You've gone off the boil ever since that unfortunate accident with the macchiato."

"What are you saying?" Joshua said. His face had gone completely white. He looked like he was about to faint.

"I'm saying you're fired."

"NO!" Joshua exclaimed, leaping up and then wincing as he landed on his cast.

He hobbled toward Elliot, his hands clasped in prayer position. The entire writing staff sat watching with open mouths. No one could quite believe what they were witnessing, a grown man groveling for his job. The despot had finally been brought to his knees.

"Heather, can you arrange for security to escort Josh off the premises?" Elliot said calmly.

Keira felt a surge of satisfaction.

Then Elliot looked at Keira. "I have a new assignment for you. For you both," he added, looking at Nina. "You clearly work well as a team. Would you please join me in my office?"

Keira looked over at Nina, surprised by the turn of events. They left Joshua in a heap on the meeting room floor and walked past the staring eyes of the junior writers into Elliot's office.

"Please, take a seat," Elliot said.

Everyone sat.

"Keira, I'm impressed with your work. It takes a lot of guts to go against the grain. The Love Letter of Lisdoonvarna article is fast becoming our most read piece. The viewing figures are going through the roof! Our readers love it. I love it!"

Heather laid a piece of paper onto the table. It was a graph. "Our usual average viewings are this line," she said, pointing to one that showed a steady upward trend. "This is Keira's piece." She pointed at the red line that shot right up so quickly as to be practically vertical.

"I knew that irony was out," Elliot said. "Didn't I say that? It's all about sincerity these days. I don't know how I let Joshua convince me otherwise. Good thing someone here knows what they're doing."

Keira smiled with pride. "Thanks." This wasn't what she'd been expecting at all. She didn't know how to react.

"I want you to keep this up," Elliot said. "Make it a regular feature. Four-page centerfolds for each monthly issue. A different romantic location. What do you say?"

Keira blinked, shocked. "You want me to travel again?"

He nodded. "I'll draw up a list of locations. Paris. Rome. Valencia. How does that sound?"

Keira could hardly catch her breath. "It sounds like a dream come true."

"Wonderful," Elliot said. "Of course we'll negotiate a high fee going forward. If you'd be willing to accept this for the time being before we finalize the new figures that would be appreciated."

He slid two pieces of paper across the table, one for Keira and one for Nina. Keira picked hers up and saw it was a check. A check for $5,000! By the sound of Nina's gasp she could tell her friend had received an equally exciting bonus check.

Keira new immediately what she was going to spend her money on. Flights for Shane to come and visit her!

"Now I imagine you'll be wanting a bit of a break following your hard work on the Ireland piece," Elliot continued. "So let's schedule some time in the next week or so to talk about the new assignment. Heather can see to that."

Feeling triumphant and more powerful than ever, Keira nodded her agreement. She couldn't believe what was happening. Her honesty had taken her to a place she'd never anticipated, somewhere beyond her wildest dreams!

And the best gift of all was that she'd be able to see Shane again, sooner than either of them had anticipated. She swirled out of Elliot's office feeling over the moon and as light as a feather.

EPILOGUE

Three thousand miles away, Shane entered the St. Paddy's Inn.

"Orin? Where are you?" he called out.

The bar man appeared from the store room. "Morning, Shane. I thought you'd have left Lisdoonvarna by now. Want to have breakfast?"

Shane agreed and Orin put some bread in the toaster.

"Keira's article has gone live," Shane told Orin. "Look."

He showed the elderly man the *Viatorum* magazine website, where the Love Letter to Lisdoonvarna was proudly displayed. The comment section was now running into the thousands. The piece had been shared a multitude of times.

"Fabulous," Orin gushed. "Look, there's us!"

He pointed at one of the candid shots Keira had had Nina include, the one of her, Shane, and Orin at the bar on her last night in Ireland.

"She's raving about the B&B," Shane said. "And the festival."

Just then, Orin's phone rang. He answered it. Shane listened to his half of the conversation curiously. When Orin was finished he sat back down.

"A booking," he said. "From an American lady who wants to attend next year's festival."

Shane looked surprised. "She's planning a bit far in advance, isn't she?"

Orin nodded. "She said she wanted to get a room before they all sell out." He chuckled. Shane laughed too. The B&B had never been fully booked in its entire history of existence!

Orin went to take a bite of his toast when the phone rang again. He looked puzzled as he went to answer it. Shane listened in again, aware that Orin was taking another booking.

Orin came back looking even more surprised than before. "Another booking from America," he said.

Shane beamed. "This must be because of Keira's article!" he said.

"I think you're right," Orin replied. The phone started to ring again. He leapt up eagerly this time and hurried off to answer the call.

Shane felt overjoyed by what was happening. Orin deserved it, he'd worked hard all his life. He felt incredibly grateful to Keira for making that change happen.

He realized then just how much he missed her. Contact between them since she'd left had been minimal. Just a message to say she was home safe. He hadn't wanted to bombard her but to give her space to readjust to New York life. Now he wasn't sure if he could keep holding off. He desperately wanted to speak to her, even if only to congratulate her on the success of the piece.

While Orin was busy taking booking after booking, Shane decided to call Keira.

"Oh hi, Mr. Lisdoonvarna," she said brightly when she answered the call. "I was about to call you."

"You were?" he replied. "The Queen of the Burren wanted to call lowly old me?"

"Yes," she replied, giggling. "My article has gone live. I thought you might want to read it."

"Already have," Shane said. "It's brilliant. And Orin's phone has been ringing off the hook all morning with bookings."

"Really?" Keira exclaimed. "That's wonderful news!"

"That's why I was calling, actually," Shane said. "I wanted to congratulate you. Everyone's buzzing about the article online. You deserve it."

"Thanks," Keira replied in a sunny voice.

Shane suddenly found himself lost for words. He felt like he should ask her how New York City was treating her, how she was doing camping out on Bryn's couch. But instead, he realized there was only one thing he wanted to say.

"Keira, I love you."

There was a long pause. "You do?"

"Yes," Shane said, and he realized he hadn't felt this certain about anything for a very long time. Since Deidre, even. "I can't stop thinking about you. I miss you like crazy. I know we sort of spoke about carrying on once you went home without really deciding, but I think we can make it work. If I save up enough money to, can I come and see you in New York City?"

"Actually," Keira began, and Shane felt a crushing sensation in his chest. She was going to turn him down. Of course she was. For her, this was just a fun little fling in a foreign country. He'd been an idiot to think it was real.

She continued. "You might not need to save up at all."

Shane paused, frowning with confusion. "I don't get it."

"My boss gave me a bonus," Keira said. "Enough to fly you out to New York. I have a week off. What do you think?"

Shane almost dropped the phone with surprise. "You can't spend your hard-earned bonus on me. It wouldn't be right."

"Would you feel less guilty if I told you it would only be about fifteen percent of what I was given?"

Shane couldn't believe it. Keira must have been given a hefty bonus if flights to New York City from Ireland were such a small percentage of it! He still felt bad about accepting it, but at the same time, there was more than one way he could think of to repay the favor.

"Well, the festival's over," he said. "There's nothing in the way of employment keeping me in Ireland at the moment."

"Is that a yes?" Keira asked, brightly.

Shane felt a tingle of excitement race through him. He could hardly believe what he was hearing. "You really want me to come to New York?" he asked. "This isn't a trick?"

Keira laughed, her voice like a tinkling bell. "No trick! Shane, there's nothing more I want in the entire world. I love you and miss you like crazy too. It's kind of unbearable. So, what do you say?"

Shane exhaled the breath that had stuck in his lungs. The thought of reuniting with Keira filled him with joy and excitement. "Yes. Yes, of course!"

"Then it's a date," Keira replied.

WILL BE AVAILABLE SOON!

LOVE LIKE THAT
(The Romance Chronicles—Book 2)

"Sophie Love's ability to impart magic to her readers is exquisitely wrought in powerfully evocative phrases and descriptions….[This is] the perfect romance or beach read, with a difference: its enthusiasm and beautiful descriptions offer an unexpected attention to the complexity of not just evolving love, but evolving psyches. It's a delightful recommendation for romance readers looking for a touch more complexity from their romance reads."
--*Midwest Book Review* (Diane Donovan re: *For Now and Forever*)

"A very well written novel, describing the struggle of a woman to find her true identity. The author did an amazing job with the creation of the characters and her description of the environment. The romance is there, but not overdosed. Kudos to the author for this amazing start of a series that promises to be very entertaining."
--*Books and Movies Reviews*, Roberto Mattos (re: *For Now and Forever)*

LOVE LIKE THAT (The Romance Chronicles—Book #2) is book #2 in a new romance series by #1 bestselling author Sophie Love.

Keira Swanson, 28, returns to New York, her head spinning from her Ireland trip and still madly in love with Shane. But when a surprise event comes between them, their relationship may have to end.

Keira is a star at her magazine, though, and they give her their next plum assignment: to travel to Italy for 30 days and discover what the Italian secret is to love.

Keira, still reeling from her Ireland trip, finds her high expectations for Italy dashed, as nothing at first goes as was planned. In her whirlwind trip through Italy, spanning Naples, the Amalfi Coast, Capri, Rome, Verona, Venice and Florence, Keira begins to wonder if the Italians really do hold a secret to love.

That is, until she meets her new tour guide—and everything she thought she knew is turned on its head.

A whirlwind romantic comedy that is as profound as it is funny, LOVE LIKE THAT is book #2 in a dazzling new romance series that will make you laugh, cry, and will keep you turning pages late into the night—and will make you fall in love with romance all over again.

Book #3 will be published soon!

Sophie Love

#1 bestselling author Sophie Love is author of the romantic comedy series, THE INN AT SUNSET HARBOR, which includes six books (and counting), and which begins with FOR NOW AND FOREVER (THE INN AT SUNSET HARBOR—BOOK 1).

Sophie Love is also the author of the debut romantic comedy series, THE ROMANCE CHRONICLES, which begins with LOVE LIKE THIS (THE ROMANCE CHRONICLES—BOOK 1).

Sophie would love to hear from you, so please visit www.sophieloveauthor.com to email her, to join the mailing list, to receive free ebooks, to hear the latest news, and to stay in touch!

CPSIA information can be obtained
at www.ICGtesting.com
Printed in the USA
LVHW010507170522
718907LV00011B/1558